(11544)

125-

28646
8-3-88

D0982514

FILES ON PARADE

Also by John O'Hara

APPOINTMENT IN SAMARRA

THE DOCTOR'S SON,
AND OTHER STORIES

BUTTERFIELD 8

HOPE OF HEAVEN

FILES on PARADE

BY JOHN O'HARA

Harcourt, Brace and Company   New York

COPYRIGHT, 1939, BY

HARCOURT, BRACE AND COMPANY, INC.

*All rights reserved, including
the right to reproduce this book
or portions thereof in any form.*

first edition

RARE
PS
3529
.H29
F55
1939

Designed by Robert Josephy

PRINTED IN THE UNITED STATES OF AMERICA
BY QUINN & BODEN COMPANY, INC., RAHWAY, N. J.

TO

KATHARINE DELANEY O'HARA

WHOSE SON I AM

Acknowledgment is here made to the editors of *The New Yorker* and *Harper's Bazaar* for permission to reprint stories first published in their pages.

Foreword

A NY BOOKSELLER or publisher will tell you, without giving the matter a thought, that books of short stories do not sell, yet the publishers go on publishing them, and I am very glad they do. I would hate to think I could not reread and reread Ring Lardner, Ernest Hemingway, Dorothy Parker, F. Scott Fitzgerald, Conan Doyle, H. H. Munro, some of William Saroyan, some of Guy de Maupassant. Whether you like it or not, I like to reread some of my own short pieces, and if they did not get into books, I never could reread them because I never have saved a clipping or a carbon copy of anything I ever wrote. Lardner never published a novel, neither did Dorothy Parker, nor, so far as I know, did Saki, Saroyan, or Maupassant; so it's a good thing for my pleasure that publishers do publish books of short stories. We all know that some of the best of Hemingway is in short stories, but there are too many persons who do not know, for instance, "All the Sad Young Men." And what about "These Thirteen"? That book, and the novel "Light in August" are my favorite Faulkner books. I am not holding the publishers' coats, but I am glad they had the artistic integrity to bring out the collections of the above-mentioned writers. Just incidentally I wouldn't mind having the publishers' profit on "Round-Up," "Men Without Women," "After Such Pleasures," and "The Adventures of Sherlock Holmes."

I like to write (sure, I know that's supposed to be a terrible admission), I like to see my stuff in print, I like my own by-line. (If I didn't like to write I would get the hell out of this kind of writing and do some other kind of writing or do some completely different kind of work.) Therefore I like this book and am glad it is being published. As to this Foreword, I never wrote a preface or an introduction for myself or anyone else, and I often have wanted to. This one —as the reader surely will have suspected—is a fairly cagey way of acknowledging to the above-mentioned writers the pleasure I have had, and hope to renew, in *their* books of short stories.

J. O'H.

Contents

FILES ON PARADE

Price's Always Open

THE PLACE where everybody would end up before going home was Price's. This was the second summer for Price's. Before that it had been a diner and an eyesore. The last man to run the diner had blown town owing everybody, and somehow or other that had put a curse on the place. No one, not even the creditors, wanted to open up again, and time and the weather got at the diner and for two years it had stood there, the windows all smashed by passing schoolboys, the paint gone, and the diner itself sagging in the middle like an old work horse. Then last summer Mr. Price got his bonus and he went into the all-night-restaurant business.

The first thing he did was to get permission to tear down the diner and put up his own place. It was a corner plot, and he built his place twice as wide as the diner had been. The Village Fathers were only too glad to have Mr. Price build. In other times they never would have let the place go the way the diner had. The neatness of the village was always commented upon by new summer people and bragged about by those who had been coming there for generations. But things being the way they were . . . So Mr. Price built a sort of rustic place, which, while not in keeping with the rest of the village architecture, was clean and attractive in its way. All the signboards were simulated shingles, and the lettering has been described as quaint. Mr. Price frankly admitted he got his idea from a chain of places in New York. There was one neon sign that stayed on all night, and it said, simply, "PRICE's." Nothing about what Price's was; everyone knew.

Mr. Price had one leg, having left the other somewhere in a dressing station back of Château-Thierry. He was not a cook but a house painter, and he had had to employ a couple of short-order cooks from New York and Boston. But Mr. Price was always there. Not that anyone ever wondered about it, but it might have been interesting to find out just when he slept. He was at his position near the cash register all night, and he certainly was there at noon when the chauffeurs and a few summer-hotel clerks and people like that would come in for lunch. As a matter of fact, he did not need much sleep. No day passed without his leg bothering him, and seeing people took his mind off his leg. Best of all, he liked late at night.

Saturday night there was always a dance at the yacht club. That was a very late crowd. The dances were supposed to stop at one, but if the stricter older members had gone home, the young people would keep the orchestra for another hour or two, and even after that they would hang around while one of the boys played the piano. The boy who played the piano was Jackie Girard.

They were a nice bunch of kids, practically all of them, and Mr. Price had known their fathers and mothers for years, or many of them. Sometimes the wife's family had been coming to this island for years and years; then she married the husband, a stranger, and the husband and wife would start coming here and keep coming. Sometimes it was the husband who was old summer people. Most of the present younger crowd had been coming here every summer for fifteen, twenty years. One or two of them had been born here. But Jackie Girard was Mr. Price's favorite. He was born here, and unlike the others, he lived here all year round.

Jackie had a strange life with the summer people, and it probably was that that made Mr. Price feel closer to him than to the others. The others were nice and respectful, and they always said *Mister* Price, just as Jackie did. But they were summer people, and the winters were long. Not that Jackie was here in the winter any more, but at least he came home several times in the winter. Jackie was at college at Holy Cross, and naturally his holidays were spent here.

The strange life that Jackie had apparently did not seem strange to him. He was not a member of the yacht club, naturally. Jackie's father was a carpenter, the best in the village; the best out of three, it's true, but head and shoulders above the other two. Henry Girard was a French Canuck and had been in the Twenty-sixth Division with Mr. Price, but never an intimate of Mr. Price's. Jackie had three sisters; one older, two younger. Jackie's mother played the organ in the Catholic church. The older sister was married and lived in Worcester, and the younger ones were in high school. Anyway, Jackie was not a member of the yacht club, but he was almost always sure of being invited to one of the dinners before the regular Saturday-night dance. He was one of the clerks at the hotel, and that, plus an occasional five or ten from his sister in Worcester, gave him just enough money to pay for gas and his incidental expenses. He could hold his end up. The only trouble was, except for Saturday and Sunday, he did not have much end to hold up.

There were gatherings, if not parties, practically every night of the week. Every Thursday, for instance, the large group of young people would split up into smaller groups, sometimes three, four, five, and after dinner they would go to the boxing matches. Jackie was not invited to these small dinner parties. He had been invited two or three times, but his mother had told him he had better not go. For herself, she wished he could have gone, but his father would not have approved. After Jackie had regretted the few invitations he got, the summer people figured it out that all he cared about was the yacht-club dances. He was the only town boy who was invited to yacht-club dances, and they figured that that was all he wanted. It did not take them long to decide that this was as it should be all around. They decided that Jackie would feel embarrassed at the smaller parties, but that he did not need to feel embarrassed at the club dances, because in a sense he was earning his way by playing such perfectly marvelous piano. But this was not the way Mr. Price saw it.

Almost every night but Saturday Jackie would drop in. Two nights a week he had been to the movies, which changed twice a week, but Mr. Price at first wondered what Jackie would do to kill time the other nights.

Jackie would show up around eleven-thirty and sit at the counter until some of the summer crowd began to arrive. They would yell at him, "Hi, Jackie! Hi, keed! How's it, Jackie?" And Jackie would swing around on his stool, and they would yell at him to come on over and sit at a table with them. And he would sit at the table with whichever group arrived first. In the early part of the summer that did not mean any special group, because when the other groups would arrive, they would put all the tables together and form one party. Then there would be some bickering about the bill, and more than once Mr. Price saw Jackie grab the check for the whole party. It was not exactly a big check; you could not eat much more than forty cents' worth at Mr. Price's without making a pig of yourself, and the usual order was a cereal, half-milk-half-cream, and a cup of coffee; total, twenty cents. But you take fourteen of those orders and you have a day's pay for Jackie.

As the summer passed, however, the large group did break into well-defined smaller groups; one of six, several of four. By August there would be the same foursomes every night, and of these one included the Leech girl.

The Leeches were not old people in the sense that

some of them were. The Leeches belonged to the new-comers who first summered in this place in 1930 and 1931. They had come from one of the more famous resorts. Louise Leech was about twelve when her family first began to come to this place. But now she was eighteen or nineteen. She had a Buick convertible coupé. She was a New York girl, whereas most of the other boys and girls were not New Yorkers; they all went to the same schools and colleges, but they did not come from the same home towns. Some came from as far west as Denver, as Mr. Price knew from cashing their checks. And even what few New York girls did come to this place were not New York friends of the Leeches. Mr. Leech was here only on week-ends and his wife was away most of the time, visiting friends who had not had to give up Narragansett. Louise herself was away a good deal of the time.

It was easy to see, the first summer Louise was grown up, that she was discontented. She did not quite fit in with the rest of the crowd, and she not only knew it but she was content not to make the best of it. Mr. Price could hear the others, the first summer he was in business, making remarks about Louise and her thinking she was too good for this place. And they had been saying something like it the early part of this summer, too. But after the Fourth of July, somewhere around there, they began to say better things about her. Mostly they said she really wasn't so bad when you got to know her. To which a few of the girls said, "Who wants to?" And others said, "She doesn't like us any better. We're still not good enough for her. But Sandy is." Which did explain a lot.

Sandy—Sandy Hall—was from Chicago, but what with prep school and college and this place and vacation trips, he probably had not spent a hundred days in Chicago in the last seven years. In a bathing suit he was almost skinny, except for his shoulders; he looked cold, he was so thin. But Mr. Price had seen him in action one night when one of the Portuguese fishermen came in drunk and got profane in a different way from the way the summer people did. Sandy had got up and let the Portuguese have two fast hard punches in the face, and the fisherman went down and stayed down. Sandy looked at the man on the floor—it was hard to tell how long he looked at him—and suddenly he kicked him. The man was already out, and so there was no need to kick him, but the kick had several results. One was that Mr. Price brought a blackjack to work the next night. The other result was something Mr. Price noticed on Louise's face.

He had not had much time to take it all in, as he had had to leave the cash register to help the night counterman drag the fisherman out of the place. But he remembered the expression on the girl's face. It began to appear when the fisherman went down from the punches, and when Sandy kicked the man, it was all there. Mr. Price, standing where he did, was the only one who caught it. He thought of it later as the way a girl would look the first time she saw Babe Ruth hit a home run, provided she cared about home runs. Or the way she would look if someone gave her a bucketful of diamonds. And other ways, that would come with experiences that Mr. Price was sure Louise never had had.

Sandy had not come with Louise that night, but Mr. Price noticed she went home with him. And after that night they were always together. They were part of a foursome of whom the other two were the dullest young people in the crowd. It took Mr. Price some time to determine why this was, but eventually he did figure it. The foursome would come into Price's, and Louise and Sandy would watch the others while they ordered; then Sandy would say he and Louise wanted the same, and from then on neither Sandy nor Louise would pay any attention to the other two. Stooges.

Another thing that Mr. Price noticed was that Jackie could not keep his eyes off Louise.

Along about the latter part of August, it was so obvious that one night Mr. Price kidded Jackie about it. It was one of the nights Jackie dropped in by himself, and Mr. Price said, "Well, she isn't here yet."

"Who isn't here?"

"The Leech girl."

"Oh," said Jackie. "Why, did anybody say anything to you? Is that how you knew I liked her?"

"No. Figured it out for myself. I have eyes."

"You're a regular Walter Winchell. But don't say anything, Mr. Price."

"What the hell would I say, and who to?"

"I'll be back," said Jackie. He was gone for more than an hour, and when he returned the crowd was there. They all yelled as usual, but this time one of the girls added, "Jackie's tight." He was, rather. He had a somewhat silly grin on his face, and his nice teeth made a line from ear to ear. Several tables wanted him to join them and they were friendly about it. But he went to the table where sat Louise and Sandy and the others.

"Do you mind if I sit down?" he said.

"Do you mind?" said Sandy.

"No," said Louise.

"Thank you. Thank you," said Jackie. "Go fights?"

"Mm-hmm," said Sandy.

"Any good? Who won?"

"The nigger from New Bedford beat the townie," said Sandy. "Kicked the Jesus out of him."

"Oh, uh townie. You mean Bobbie Lawless. He's nice guy. Za friend of mine. I used to go to high school—"

"He's yellow," said Sandy.

"Certainly was," said Louise.

"Nope. Not yellow. Not Bobbie. I used to go to high school with Bobbie. Plain same football team."

"Where do you go to school now?" said Sandy.

"Holy Cross. We're gonna beat you this year."

"What is Holy Cross?" said Louise.

Sandy laughed. Jackie looked at her with tired eyes.

"No, really, what is it?"

" 'Tsa college. It's where I go to college. Dint you ever hear of Holy Cross? Give another hoya and a choo-choo rah rah—"

"O.K.," said Sandy.

"I'll sing if I wanta. I'll sing one of your songs. Oh, hit the line for Harvard, for Harvard wins today—"

"Oh, go away," said Sandy.

"Yes, for God's *sake*," said Louise.

"Oh, very well, Miss Leech. Very well." Jackie put his hands on the table to steady himself as he got to his feet, but he stared down into her eyes and for two seconds he was sober.

"Come on, Jackie, you're stewed." Mr. Price had come around from the cash register and had taken Jackie by the right arm. At that moment Sandy lashed out with a right-hand punch, and Jackie fell down. But he had hardly reached the floor before Mr. Price snapped his blackjack from his pocket and slapped it down on the front of Sandy's head. Sandy went down and there was blood.

"Anybody else?" said Mr. Price. By this time the night counterman had swung himself over the counter, and in his hand was a baseball bat, all nicked where it had been used for tamping down ice around milk cans. None of the summer crowd made a move; then Mr. Price spoke to two of the young men. "Get your friend outa here, and get out, the whole goddam bunch of you." He stood where he was, he and the counterman, and watched the girls picking up their wraps.

"Aren't you going to do anything?" Louise screamed. "Chuck! Ted! All of you!"

"You get out or I'll throw you out," said Mr. Price. She left.

There were murmurs as well as the sounds of the cars starting. Thinking it over, Mr. Price agreed with himself that those would be the last sounds he ever expected to hear from the summer crowd.

Trouble in 1949

ARRY came out of the local skyscraper and stood
on the sidewalk and took a long look at his watch,
just as the Midwestern heat hit him in the face. Rutland, in his air-conditioned office, had kept him just long
enough so that to make the last good New York plane
he would have to hurry and sweat—and then probably
miss it. He walked to the hotel and took a shower, not
hot and not cold, which made him feel better if not
cooler. He sent downstairs for the largest Tom Collins
they could provide, and he sat in a pongee dressing
gown, sipping his drink and glancing at a picture magazine and smoking a cigarette. He sent down for another
Tom Collins, and stood at the window, trying to test
his memory. That building was new; and that one.
That one that looked like the roof of a movie house,
he wasn't sure whether that was new. It had been a
long time. Eleven years, almost.

"Before he knew what he was doing, he had the
phone book in his hand," he said to himself, of himself,
and added: "And what a liar you are, Barry." He had

been lying to himself for three days, ever since he knew he was coming out here. He had lied to Rutland, who had said: "Listen, Barry, what's the use of trying to catch that plane? Why don't you wait here a few minutes and we can go over to the H-Y-P Club and have a couple of snorts. They have an air-conditioned bar. Then we can drive out to the country club and have a swim. There'll be a lot of pretty girls out there. All the young kids. Then we can either have dinner there or go to my house. Let me call my wife and tell her you're coming." But he had told Rutland that he couldn't possibly. He *had* to be back in New York first thing in the morning.

That was a lie. He wanted to go to the H-Y-P Club; there would be guys there he knew and had not seen. He wanted to go for a swim. But he knew that country club, and he knew who might be there.

He found her name in the phone book, or rather her husband's name. He called the number: "May I speak to Mrs. Nelson?"

"Yessuh, Mistah Nelson. Just one minute."

Then: "Hello, Karl?"

"No, this isn't Karl. This is Jock Barry."

A silence that made him begin to think he was cut off, and then: "Jock? What are you doing in these parts?" And before he could answer she added: "Or are you in these parts?"

"Yes, I'm at the Deshler."

"Well, then you're not in these parts. The Deshler is in Columbus, Ohio."

"Well, whatever the name of it is."

"The Imperial, most likely," she said. "How long are you going to be here?"

He noticed that the invitation to dinner which he had been expecting was slow in coming, if it was coming. "I'm going back to New York tomorrow."

"Well, in that case you must come out for dinner. Karl won't be here for dinner, I'm afraid, but he'll be back later."

"Oh, that's too bad."

"What's too bad?" she said.

"I leave that to you," he said. "Look, why don't you have dinner with me?"

"At the Imperial? I wouldn't think of it. Drive four miles to sit in—oh, no, thanks."

"I didn't say it had to be the Imperial. There must be some place in the country. There used to be lots of places."

"There still are, but when I go to them I go with Karl."

"I see," he said, and deliberately waited.

"How is Connie?" she asked.

"She's fine. She's in Maine. Shall I give her your love?"

Now it was she who waited. "I'll be there in about an hour. Meet me at the State Street entrance. It's a light blue convertible coupé. More's the pity," she said.

"We can put it in a garage and hire a drive-yourself," he said, but she had hung up.

He took a small steel mirror out of his shaving kit and went to the window, examining his beard and trying to give it the benefit of a doubt; but it was no go, and so he shaved. The waiter arrived with the second Tom Collins and Barry told him to see about having his other suit pressed. In half an hour he inspected himself in the full-length mirror. Not really so bad. If he pulled his chin back it doubled a little, and there was the beginning of a faint suspicion of a tiny bulge over his collar; but when he held his chin up the double and the bulge disappeared. "Chin up, mahst dress," he quoted from Bert Lahr. He buttoned the three buttons on his coat, made an unnecessary rearrangement of his tie, put on his straw hat at an angle, and with a Maurice Chevalier tap of the crown he made a face at himself: "Eef da nighteengales cood sing glike yoo, dey'd sing motch sweedah dan dey do." He went downstairs, to the State Street entrance of the Imperial Hotel. He almost wished he had a bamboo walking stick.

At ten minutes past the hour of seven a medium-sized blue convertible coupé turned into State Street, half a block away. He darted between the battling taxi-cabs and jumped to the running board. "Hello," she said, and looked at him only once, as though she had not seen him since lunch, and not a very romantic lunch either. He got in. He leaned forward and very exaggeratedly pretended to be dazzled. "Now don't be silly," she said. "And don't tell me I haven't changed. You have. You better get out of this town before the meat packers see you."

"Oh, now really, Mrs. Nelson. You don't have to work so hard at it."

"At what, pray?"

"At being the happily wed Mrs. Nelson, Mrs. Nelson." He pretended to quote: "Mrs. Karl J. Nelson—"

"Karl W."

"Mrs. Karl Q. Nelson, one of our most attractive young matrons, who is chairman of the bird-bath committee of the Junior League, pictured with her twelve interesting children at her home on Ridgewood Place.

Mrs. Nelson is the former, uh, the former, uh. Now what was the name? What—was—that—name? Everyone seems to have forgotten it, including Mrs. Nelson. Excepting Mr. J. J. Barry, of New York. He remembers when Mrs. Nelson was a Miss Judy Hayes. Does he remember!"

"Well, forget it. She's Mrs. Nelson now, all evening, too. We can go to a place called the Château, where they have a waiter that used to be at 21, if that'll make you homesick. I understand they have excellent wines, and I know the food is good. I don't imagine wine interests you any more than it ever did."

"Or did you."

"Or did me. They have a four-piece band, not bad. We can have dinner, dance once or twice around, and be home in plenty of time for the historic meeting between you and Karl. He hates you."

"I'd be pretty sore if he didn't."

"Do you want to drive?" she asked.

"Yes."

"As soon as we get out of this traffic," she said. They changed seats, and at that there was a subtler change. He felt more in control of the situation when he had his hands on the wheel and the responsibility of the car; and apparently some change had affected her.

"Bear right. Left at the next light. The cops are always hanging around this gas station." That was all she said for the first few minutes, then: "It's funny I never ran into you somewhere."

"You never tried," he said.

"No, but I never tried not to," she said. He turned, but she was staring straight ahead, and he knew she expected him to turn, and then when his eyes were back on the road he knew she was smiling at him.

"Hello, Judy," he said.

"Hello, Jock," she said, and as he reached his hand toward her she came closer.

"Don't some people named McAllister live out this way?"

"McPherson."

"They have a herd of cattle," he said.

"Champion Jerseys," she said.

"I thought so," he said.

The Château was not near. It turned out to be a good twenty miles from the hotel, but it was a good twenty miles. Barry held her hand, and they had only one more conversation before they arrived at the roadhouse. She began it: "Are you confused, Jock?"

"Yes, darling. I'm confused. Why?"

"I am. It's no use pretending we're the same, because we're not. I weigh a hundred and twenty-seven, and you must weigh— I don't know men's weights very well. I'm three years younger than you are, so that makes you thirty-four, doesn't it?"

"Yep. That makes you thirty-one. You thirty-one!"

"Yes, and you thirty-four."

"Yes, but you thirty-one! You thirty-anything, Judy. Why are you confused?"

"I'm not actually, all of a sudden. Time marches on, and I have two children. You have two children. You have a wife, and I have a husband. But I feel only very slightly disloyal to all that. To them. And you? What about you?"

"Only very slightly."

"Because I loved you when I didn't know anything except that I loved you. So let's have a good time to-night? Let's accept it that you aren't twenty-three and I'm not twenty. We'll accept it and forget it."

"Yes, that's what I want." And with the effect of that agreement still on them they arrived at the Château, so-called no doubt for the reason that it resembled no château in the world. He stopped the car to let her out. She put a hand on the door and then she turned and put her arms around his neck and kissed him.

"That's all for now, darling. I'll meet you in the

bar." She got out and he waited until she was inside. For a second he found himself not liking, not caring about the girl of eleven years ago; but very much in love with this woman in the brown-and-white sport shoes and white gabardine dress. He admired the way her beautiful legs took her up the porch steps. There was even something about the way she opened the screen door. Or maybe it was only that it was she who was opening the screen door. He parked the car and found the bar.

It was a pleasant bar. One look at the saintly white-haired Irish bartender and he knew that it was a good bar, an efficient bartender. Probably one of those bachelor bartenders who spend their time going from Florida to New York to Saratoga, going on two or three benders a year, winning a little on the races, losing a little, and then taking jobs at places like the Château to recoup their losses. It was the kind of bar which would be a good place for a small group, or an equally good place to drink alone, for the entire back bar was stocked with bottles—labels to read.

There was one other couple at the bar. A man about Barry's age; a woman about Judy's age.

"Good evening, sir," said the bartender.

"Good evening. I think I'll wait just a minute."

"Yes, sir." The bartender brought him a glass of ice water and Judy came in from Mesdames.

"Hello, Judy," said the man.

"Oh, hello, Paul," she said. The two women did not speak.

"What are you going to drink?" said Barry.

They decided on Martinis, and the bartender sent for the waiter. They ordered: melon, chicken Château (chicken hash, ham, and grapes). And champagne. Be ready as soon as they cared to sit down. They ordered a second cocktail to be sent to the table, and when they sat down she said: "Paul, the man at the bar, in case you're interested, is my brother-in-law. Karl's brother."

"Well, isn't that nice? But I don't think that's his wife."

"No, it isn't. Nobody blames Paul, though. At least I don't. His wife is racketing around with a football player from the University. His wife has the money."

"What about your husband? Wouldn't he help him?"

"No. Karl says he's lost respect for him. They don't get along very well. You know, I'm rather hungry."

The food, what there was of it, was good, and the wine was acceptable. The owner of the place came to their table and asked if everything was satisfactory, and they said it was, but where was the orchestra. The Basque shrugged his shoulders and apologetically explained that he could only afford the band on week-ends this summer. When the man had bowed himself away Paul Nelson succeeded him. He bowed to Barry and said, "Excuse me, Judy—"

"It's all right. Paul, this is Mr. Barry, from New York. My brother-in-law, Mr. Nelson."

They shook hands and Barry asked him to sit down. Nelson said he would and then, addressing Barry: "Do you mind if I speak frankly?"

"Notta tall, if you're asking me," said Barry.

"What is it, Paul?"

"Judy," said Nelson, "if I were you, I mean, I think it would be a good idea if you finished your drinks and got out of here. Karl's coming here with a crowd of men."

"How do you know?" said Judy.

Paul smiled. "Because Luigi gave me the same tip. When I first got here he told me, 'Ah, Mr. Nelson. Early,' and I asked him what he meant, and then he explained. He thought I was meeting my brother here. They're all coming from the plant and Karl's secretary phoned and ordered dinner. Then when you and this gentleman got here Luigi called me aside and asked

if you weren't Karl's wife. So, there it is." He looked
at his watch. "They ought to be here fairly soon, and
you know Karl. Arriving here with his big business pals
and finding his wife with a stranger. I take it you don't
know Karl?"

"No, I've never met him. But thanks. I think it
would be better if we ducked, Judy."

"Yes—but it's too late now. Look at those cars."

"It isn't too late," said Paul. "You can go through
the bar and out the other end of the porch."

"No. I have my car."

"Oh, God," said Paul. "No, it isn't too late. You can
be here with me. Mr. . . . Barry can go over and sit
with the lady with me. Her name is Mrs. Jewett. She
knows all this."

"I guess that's the best thing, Jock," said Judy.

Barry joined Mrs. Jewett. "How do you do?" she
said. "This ought to be innaresting. That's Paul's
brother. He just spotted Paul and Mrs. Nelson." It
was innaresting. First, Karl the hearty host, giving the
impression of having his arms on the shoulders of seven
men, all at once; taking their orders at the bar, mem-
orizing them instantly, and repeating them to the bartender. Then turning around and spotting his brother
and his wife. (Apparently he had not recognized the

blue car.) He walked to their table, and Barry could see restrained anger in the set of Karl's shoulders. He could not see Karl's face, but he could see Judy's, and he could guess what she was saying. Something like: "If you don't trust me, you ought to trust your own brother," et cetera. Then Judy and Paul rose and left.

"Have you got a car?" said Barry to Mrs. Jewett.

"We came in Paul's. It's that little black sedan."

He got the check and paid it. They got in Paul's car and started in the direction of the city. Half a mile ahead the blue coupé was parked. Barry pulled up and got out, and Paul got out of the coupé. Barry put out his hand. "Thanks very much, Nelson," he said.

"Thanks for what? I wasn't doing it for you."

"O.K.," said Barry. "But I wasn't thanking you for myself. Get that straight."

"Go on back to New York and leave her alone," said Paul, and left him.

Barry drove slowly; he was looking for a certain road. When he came to that road he turned off the main highway, and crawled along the road for a mile or so. They had been silent all the while. He well remembered that you drove for a while past a long white fence until you reached an arch of trees. That was where he stopped, under the arch of trees. "Cigarette?" he said.

"Yes," she said. "What did Paul say to you?"

"You're sure he said something, aren't you?"

"I know he was going to. I didn't listen," she said.

"Well," Barry began, and before continuing he took a long, long inhale of his cigarette. "I'll tell you what he said, in effect. He said, 'Barry, don't you realize you're not twenty-three? You're thirty-four,' he said. He said, 'You have a wife and two children.'"

"And then I imagine he said, 'And Judy is thirty-one, and she has a husband and two children.'"

"Something like that," said Barry. "Something like that. He didn't say anything about being in love with you himself, and I didn't ask him. I didn't have to."

"Well?" she said.

"Well, what?"

"Well, aren't you going to ask me if I'm in love with him?"

"I wasn't going to, but now I guess I don't have to," he said. He looked at her, and there was something besides tears in her eyes. It wasn't one thing; it was a lot of things. There was something he had seen a long time ago, when he had said he would be good to her. But now there was something else, and he thought he knew what it was; it was the need of someone to tell, someone to tell. Then her face was on his chest, and his kiss was in her hair; and she was twenty-one again, and he was a hundred.

"He doesn't know I love him," she said. "It's all so damn much trouble, Jock." She stopped crying, and he gave her a handkerchief. "How did you happen to pick this road?" she said.

"Don't you know?"

She smiled and kissed his cheek. "I think I do, but we passed that road. It's about a mile back."

"It's about eleven years back," he said.

"Well, just so you remember this one in—1949," she said.

The next day, on the plane, he thought of the answer to that. "But I won't remember," he should have said. "It'll be too damn much trouble."

The Cold House

THE HOUSE in the country was cold, and Mrs. Carnavon sat with her hat on, her sealskin coat open, her bag in her lap, her left hand lying flat on the bag. The slight exertion—but not slight to her—of getting out of the car, stepping down, walking up the three steps of the porte-cochère, had left her breathing heavily, and the thumb of her right hand was beating against the forefinger. She had had a long nap in the car, coming up from New York. Driscoll drove so you could sleep. He had to; that was his job. She knew Driscoll, and how he would look in the mirror to see if she was asleep before he would increase his speed. Driscoll was so thoroughly trained in moderate speed that she often had had to feign sleep in order to get some place in a hurry. But today she had not had to feign sleep. Up at six-thirty, away at seven-thirty, and now it was almost time for lunch. But first a rest, a little rest. The house was very cold. Mrs. Carnavon rang for the maid.

"I didn't expect you till late afternoon," said the maid. "I'll build you a fire."

"Never mind, Anna."

"But it'll only *take* a *minute*, Ma'am. I kin——"

"No, never *mind*."

"Well, but of course if you——"

"I won't change my mind. Is the phone connected? I mean here in the house."

"No, only over the garage, where we are."

"Then will you go out and telephone the Inn and tell Mr. McCall—ask him if I could have a chop and a baked potato. Or anything. Nothing much. Cup of tea."

"I could fix you something."

"Too much trouble to start a fire. No, just tell Mr. McCall, and find out how soon he can have it."

"Of course he'll more than likely have to go out and buy it, and——"

"All right. He can go out and buy it." Mrs. Carnavon hated to be short with Anna, but Anna had the hide of an elephant. She knew that Anna would not be hurt; she watched Anna leave the room and knew that Anna was thinking: "The poor woman is all upset."

She looked out of the window and saw Anna, with

a very ugly shawl over her head and shoulders, looking rather pathetic, hurrying to the garage to telephone
Mr. McCall. Mrs. Carnavon lit a cigarette. It steadied
her a little. It steadied her body, her hands; there was
no unsteadiness to the lump in her heart, the thing in
her mind. She held the cigarette as high as her face,
taking regular, deep inhales. She idly opened a china
cigarette box on the table beside her, just tilting the
lid. There were four cigarettes in the box. She took
one out and it was as crisp as a twig. She broke it with
her fingers. It was from last summer. A cigarette that
her son could have smoked. She looked at it and saw
that it was a cigarette that Harry would *not* have
smoked; it was a brand he never had liked. But still,
when he had had a few drinks she had seen him smoking just that brand without noticing any difference.
"Mom, why do you have those things in the house?
Everybody passes them up. They're really vile. They
are. They're vile. I hate to tell you what they remind
me of." One time he had emptied all the available
boxes of that brand. But she noticed that when some
friends of his were at the house, they would ask Anna
if there didn't happen to be some of that brand—"on
the premises," one boy had said. She didn't remember

much about the boy, but she remembered that strange expression.

Now that she was here—"I came up here for something," she said aloud. Well, what? The cracked windowpane that she had noticed the first time one morning after Harry and his friends had been to a dance. Two decks of cards on the desk. The copy of *Life* magazine on the rack. The summer *Social Register*, with its warped cover curling up. She heard a screen door slam, an odd sound in this kind of weather, when the flies had died. It was Anna, of course. Anna's hands were cold; Mrs. Carnavon noticed them when Anna reached up to take off her shawl.

"He said he'd be glad to serve you in about three-quarters of an hour," said Anna. "I was right. He does have to go out and buy the chops. About three-quarters of an hour, he said. I think what he's doing, I think he wants to warm up the dining-room a little, too. You know, it was awful this winter for Mr. McCall. I don't believe he had more than two or three people there a week. A couple regulars, like salesmen, passing through, but overnight I don't believe he had more than two or three people. Just for lunch, the regulars. I don't think it paid him to keep open."

"Anna, will you go upstairs in Mr. Harry's room, there's a picture in a silver frame—"

"Of Dr. Carnavon. I have it out in our room."

"How dare you!"

"I'm sorry, Ma'am, I only meant to do the right thing. I didn't want anybody to steal—"

"You had no right to touch anything in that room. Go bring it to me!"

The tears came and Anna fled, and Mrs. Carnavon was weary of herself, flaring up at this miserable soul, who had no way of knowing that that room was not to be disturbed. No order had been given. Indeed, Mrs. Carnavon admitted that until now she had not thought of leaving that room the way it was, the way it had been all winter. It was part of her confusion, trying to find some reason for making this trip. Trying to find some excuse, she admitted, that would explain the trip to the servants, to Anna. And then, finally, finding the worst excuse of all: Anna would know she had not driven all this distance merely to take home a picture of a husband long dead. Weary, wearily, Mrs. Carnavon climbed the stairs to her son's room.

On the wall the same diamond-shaped plaque, with the clasped hands and the Greek letters; another wooden diamond, with the head of a wolf; a photo-

graph of a baseball team, with names badly printed in
white ink under the picture; a large bare spot where
there had been a reproduction which he had liked well
enough to take back to town. A magazine that he may
have read. She opened it: ". . . and it will become
increasingly apparent that the forces of Fascism are
laboring night and day . . . choice may have to be
made sooner than you expect; but no matter when it
comes, when it does come it will be sooner than you
like. . . ." A young friend, an *old* friend, of Harry's
had written that. An intense young man had come to
see her a month or so ago; he had been abroad, he had
just learned, he couldn't *believe* it. Why, he and
Harry, for eight years . . . Eight years? What about
twenty-four years? What was *eight* years? Well, for
one thing, it was eight years during which he had seen
Harry a great deal more than she had, like it or not.

Everything in this room would have to go. Those
things, those shields, those pictures, all that would have
to go. She would send them to the right people. Everything would have to go. She now saw that in the back
of her mind, as she was climbing the stairs, had been
some vague plan to lock this room and leave everything as she found it; but now when she saw this she
felt chilled and disgusted. Let him be dead, but let

him be dead! Let him be what he was, and let it have ended with no awful sanctuary or crypt of useless things. Oh, how useless were these things! "I do not even know what Upsilon means," she whispered. "Those baseball players. Do I want to see *them?*" She recoiled from the nearness of a danger, the danger of keeping this room the way it was, and the lone, secret visits she would have paid it, looking at things that had no meaning to her. She could see clearly, like watching a motion picture of herself, what she would have done, what she had been in terrible danger of doing: next August, next September, a year from next August and a year from next July, she would have come up here, unlocked the door, come in this room and stood. She saw herself, a woman in white, trying to squeeze out a tear at the sight of these things of wood and brass and paper and glass—and all the while distracted by the sounds of passing cars, the children next door, the telephone downstairs, the whirring vacuum cleaner. And she even knew the end of this motion picture: she would end by hating a memory that she only knew how to love.

She walked out, leaving the door open, and went downstairs. Anna was standing in the hall, with fear in her eyes. Mrs. Carnavon looked at her watch. "Tell Driscoll to bring the car around."

"He's having a bite with us," said Anna.

"Tell him to bring that *car* around!" said Mrs. Carnavon. "I'm going back by train."

The train was quicker.

Days

Aᴼᴛᴇʀ the first few days there the habits of living in a new place began to form. Larkin would lean over and kiss his wife good-by, get out of the car, go inside the station, buy his paper at the news-stand, walk through the station, and stand out there waiting for the train. He liked to get that much air anyway, and that was how he began to notice her.

She, he found, would come out of the large apartment house, the last building before you got to the station. She walked across the graveled space and did not go inside the station at all, not even on rainy days. He had been in the town only a few weeks, and so he did not know whether she stayed inside the station when it was snowing, but from the beginning he was pretty sure she stayed outside, winter and summer.

She carried her paper under her arm. It seemed part of the general neatness of her gloved hands, her bag, her tailored clothes, the scarf at her throat, and even the way she held her head. The paper probably was the one she had delivered at her apartment, because he never saw her buy a paper at the news-stand. On that theory, one day in New York he lingered after everyone had got out of the train, and went back and picked up her paper, hoping it would have her name penciled on top, the way some newsdealers do; but the only mark on the paper was 9-H, obviously the number of her apartment. He felt ashamed that day, and terrified that the conductor, who would have recognized him, would come in and see him at a seat so far forward of the one he always tried to get. He always, after the first week or so, tried to sit behind her so that if she turned her head he could see her profile. She seldom turned her head.

The other habits were merely habits, but there was one of which he was conscious: the habit of knowing all through breakfast and before it that he would see her. In a way it was awful, to be so excited about so little, but it made the mornings good, even some bad Monday mornings after golf tournaments. The excitement would be there until she appeared, then a sort of relief, and, in the train, actual comfort. Yes, comfort, he told himself. The way he wanted to be with her; sort of like being in the same comfortable room, quietly reading, knowing she was there. But then once they were in New York, once people began getting up in the car, it would be different, a different kind of excitement that was not good, but upset him. He knew her path to the subway, and on the way she would pass tunnels that led to hotels. What if he could meet her and then some morning they could take the train as they always did, but this one morning she would turn in at one of those tunnels and wait for him, and they could go to the hotel together?

He would wonder how he could get to meet her. It was too large a suburb, too many people got on the train, for casual good mornings with people you hadn't met. There were two country clubs, and he guessed she belonged to the smaller one, the one with a nine-hole golf course. He sometimes thought of joining that club, but he knew his wife would put her foot down. "Two country clubs?" she would say. "What do you want to join that club for? Lot of other things we could use the money for." And there were, of course, and pretty soon, when his son got home from prep school, the expenses would climb. And anyway, he had no way of knowing she even belonged to the smaller club. The apartment house in which she lived had a lot of tennis-courts, and she probably played tennis. He seldom went to the movies, and he never saw her there, but what if he did? He had a better chance of getting to know her on the train than at any damn movie, with his wife there with him.

He came home one afternoon and said, "I think we ought to have a man here. A chauffeur-gardener."

"What for?"

"We need somebody like that, and they don't cost so much. He could take me to the station in the morning in the big car and you could use him to drive around, and of course, this fellow we have now, he's only a part-time gardener and not so damn good, for that matter."

"I don't see what we need a full-time man for. It's only additional expense."

"Now listen, it wouldn't cost that much more, and we'd get a lot more out of him if we had a full-time man. When Teddy comes home and starts using the Ford all the time you'll be glad of a man to drive you in the big car. You know that yourself. I'm going to call up an agency tomorrow."

"It's your money, but I think you're silly," his wife had said. And so Larkin no longer was driven to the station by his wife. In a way, he told himself, he was doing it for her; he didn't want to stop kissing her good-by, but he didn't want to be seen kissing her by the woman, whoever she was, that he loved.

Well, there it was, acknowledged at last; something he had known all along, more than likely from the first day, when seeing her appear from behind the corner of the station had had an effect on him like— a jolt. Now he began to listen to the words of songs about love, trying to discover a voice on the radio that would be just like a voice he never had heard. In a way he began to envy the people who got into messes in the papers, although that was the last thing he wanted for either of his two women—the one he was married to, and the one he loved. "Mrs. Larkin and two detectives surprised her manufacturer husband at a morning tryst with an attractive brunette at a mid-town hotel. The woman, Mrs. Larkin said, was attired in a flimsy négligé, and was about thirty years old. She said her husband had registered under the name of Lawrence. A property settlement . . . alimony . . . custody of their one son." Hell, no! That wasn't the way Anna would do it; not the way he would have it.

Oh, no? Well, if he couldn't have it any other way, he would have it that way. When he went to the station the morning after he lay thinking these things he wanted to explain to her: "If we can't have it that way, if you love me enough, let her go ahead and do as she pleases. I'll give her all the money she wants." And then he had to laugh out loud at what he was thinking, and at that moment she turned, and there was a smile in her eyes. Two other men smiled, too, at him, this man standing alone and laughing out loud at some private joke. But *she* had smiled and it was beautiful. *She* was beautiful. And on the way in on the train he suddenly knew that now it was only a question of days. Days!

Are We Leaving Tomorrow?

IT was cool, quite cool, the way the weather is likely to be at an in-between resort when the Florida season is over but the Northern summer season has not yet begun. Every morning the tall young man and his young wife would come down the steps of the porch and go for their walk. They would go to the mounting block where the riders would start for the trails. The tall young man and his wife would stand not too close to the block, not speaking to anyone; just watching. But there might have been a little in his attitude, in his manner, of a man who felt that he was starting the riders, as though his presence there made their start official. He would stand there, hatless and tan, chin down almost to his chest, his hands dug deep in the pockets of his handsome tweed topcoat. His wife would stand beside him with her arm in his, and when she would speak to him she would put her face in front of him and look up. Almost always his answer would be a smile and a nod, or perhaps a single word that expressed all he wanted to put into words. They would

watch the riders for a while, and then they would stroll
over to the first tee of the men's golf course to watch
the golfers start off. There it would be the same: not
much talk, and the slightly superior manner or attitude. After they had watched their quota of golfers
they would go back to the porch and she would go up
to their rooms and a Negro bellboy would bring him
his papers, the *Montreal Star* and the *New York Times*.
He would sit there lazily looking at the papers, never
so interested in a news item that he would not look up
at every person who came in or went out of the hotel,
or passed his chair on the porch. He watched every car
come up the short, winding drive, watched the people
get in and out, watched the car drive away; then when
there was no human activity he would return to his
paper, holding it rather far away, and on his face and
in his eyes behind the gold-rimmed spectacles there
was always the same suspicion of a smile.

He would go to his room before lunch, and they
would come down together. After lunch, like most
everyone else, they would retire, apparently for a nap,
not to appear until the cocktail hour. They would be
the first, usually, in the small, cheery bar, and until it
was time to change for dinner he would have a highball glass, constantly refilled, in his hand. He drank

slowly, sipping teaspoonfuls at a time. In that time she might drink two light highballs while he was drinking eight. She always seemed to have one of the magazines of large format in her lap, but at these times it was she who would look up, while he hardly turned his head.

Not long after they came she began to speak to people; to bow and pass the time of day. She was a pleasant, friendly little woman, not yet thirty. Her eyes were too pretty for the rest of her face; in sleep she must have been very plain indeed, and her skin was sensitive to the sun. She had good bones—lovely hands and feet—and when she was in sweater and skirt her figure always got a second look from the golfers and riders.

Their name was Campbell—Douglas Campbell, and Sheila. They were the youngest people over fifteen in the hotel. There were a few children, but most of the guests were forty or thereabouts. One afternoon the Campbell's were in the bar and a woman came in and after hesitating at the entrance she said, "Good afternoon, Mrs. Campbell. You didn't happen to see my husband?"

"No, I didn't," said Mrs. Campbell.

The woman came closer slowly and put her hand on the back of a chair near them. "I was afraid I'd missed him," she said to no one; then suddenly she said, "Do you mind if I sit with you while he comes?"

"No, not at all," said Mrs. Campbell.

"Please do," said Campbell. He got to his feet and stood very erect. He set his glass on the little table and put his hands behind his back.

"I'm sorry I don't remember your name," said Mrs. Campbell.

"Mrs. Loomis."

Mrs. Campbell introduced her husband, who said, "Wouldn't you like a cocktail meanwhile?"

Mrs. Loomis thought a moment and said she would —a dry Daiquiri. Then Campbell sat down, picking up his drink and beginning to sip.

"I think we were the first here, as usual," said Mrs. Campbell, "so we couldn't have missed Mr. Loomis."

"Oh, it's all right. One of us is always late, but it isn't important. That's why I like it here. The general air of informality." She smiled. "I've never seen you here before. Is this your first year?"

"Our first year," said Mrs. Campbell.

"From New York?"

"Montreal," said Mrs. Campbell.

"Oh, Canadians. I met some awfully nice Canadians in Palm Beach this winter," said Mrs. Loomis. She named them off, and Mrs. Campbell said they knew them, and he smiled and nodded. Then Mrs. Loomis tried to remember the names of some other people she knew in Montreal (they turned out to have been Toronto people), and Mr. Loomis arrived.

A white-haired man, a trifle heavy and about fifty, Mr. Loomis wore young men's clothes. He was brown and heavy lidded. He had good manners. It was he who corrected his wife about the people from Montreal who actually were from Toronto. That was the first time the Loomises and the Campbells had done more than speak in passing, and Mrs. Campbell was almost gay that afternoon.

The Campbells did not come down to dinner that evening, but they were out for their stroll the next morning. Mr. Loomis waved to them at the first tee, and they waved—*she* waved, Campbell nodded. They did not appear for cocktails that afternoon. For the next few days they took their stroll, but they had their meals in their room. The next time they came to the cocktail lounge they took a small table at the side of the bar, where there was room only for the table and two chairs. No one spoke to them, but that night was one of the nights when the hotel showed movies in the ballroom, and after the movie the Loomises fell in with them and insisted on buying them a drink, just a nightcap. That was the way it was.

Mr. Loomis brought out his cigar case and offered Mr. Campbell a cigar, which was declined, and gave the orders for drinks, "Scotch, Scotch, Scotch, and a Cuba Libre." Mrs. Loomis was having the Cuba Libre. As the waiter took the order Mr. Campbell said, "And bring the bottle."

There was a fraction of a second's incredulity in Mr. Loomis's face; incredulity, or more likely doubt that he had heard his own ears. But he said, "Yes, bring the bottle." Then they talked about the picture. It had been a terrible picture, they all agreed. The Loomises said it was too bad, too, because they had crossed with the star two years ago and she had seemed awfully nice, not at all what you'd expect a movie star to be like. They all agreed that the Mickey Mouse was good, although Mr. Loomis said he was getting a little tired of Mickey Mouse. Their drinks came, and Mrs. Loomis was somewhat apologetic about her drink, but ever since she had been in Cuba she'd developed a taste for rum, always rum. "And before that gin," said Mr. Loomis. Mr. Campbell's glass was empty and he called the waiter to bring some more ice and another

Cuba Libre, and he replenished the highball glasses from the bottle of Scotch on the table.

"Now this was my idea," said Mr. Loomis.

"Only the first one," said Mr. Campbell. They let it go at that, and the ladies returned to the subject of the star of the picture, and soon Mr. Loomis joined in. They got all mixed up in the star's matrimonial record, which inevitably brought up the names of other movie stars and *their* matrimonial records. Mr. and Mrs. Loomis provided the statistics, and Mrs. Campbell would say yes or no as the statement or opinion required. Mr. Campbell sipped his drink wordlessly until the Loomises, who had been married a long time, became simultaneously aware of Mr. Campbell's silence, and they began directing their remarks at him. The Loomises were not satisfied with Mrs. Campbell's ready assents. They would address the first few words of a remark to the young wife, because she had been such a polite listener, but then they would turn to Mr. Campbell and most of what they had to say was said to him.

For a while he would smile and murmur "Mm-hmm," more or less into his glass. Then it seemed after a few minutes that he could hardly wait for them to end an item or an anecdote. He began to nod before

it was time to nod, and he would keep nodding, and
he would say, "Yes, yes, yes," very rapidly. Presently,
in the middle of an anecdote, his eyes, which had been
growing brighter, became very bright. He put down
his drink and leaned forward, one hand clasping and
unclasping the other. "And—yes—and—yes," he kept
saying, until Mrs. Loomis had finished her story. Then
he leaned farther forward and stared at Mrs. Loomis,
with that bright smile and with his breathing become
short and fast.

"Can I tell you a story?" he said.

Mrs. Loomis beamed. "Why, of course."

Then Campbell told a story. It had in it a priest,
female anatomy, improbable situations, a cuckold, un-
printable words, and no point.

Long before Campbell finished his story Loomis was
frowning, glancing at his wife and at Campbell's wife,
seeming to listen to Campbell but always glancing at
the two women. Mrs. Loomis could not look away;
Campbell was telling her the story, and he looked at
no one else. While Mrs. Campbell, the moment the
story was begun, picked up her drink, took a sip, and
put the glass on the table and kept her eyes on it until
Campbell signaled by his chuckling that the story was
at an end.

He kept chuckling and looking at Mrs. Loomis after he had finished, and then he smiled at Loomis. "Huh," came from Loomis, and on his face a muscular smile. "Well, dear," he said. "Think it's about time—"

"Yes," said Mrs. Loomis. "Thank you so much. Good night, Mrs. Campbell, and good night." Campbell stood up, erect, bowing.

When they were entirely out of the room he sat down and crossed his legs. He lit a cigarette and resumed his drinking and stared at the opposite wall. She watched him. His eyes did not even move when he raised his glass to his mouth.

"Oh," she said suddenly. "I wonder if the man is still there at the travel desk. I forgot all about the tickets for tomorrow."

"Tomorrow? Are we leaving tomorrow?"

"Yes."

He stood up and pulled the table out of her way, and when she had left he sat down to wait for her.

Portistan on the Portis

ONE NIGHT not so long ago I was having dinner with a friend of mine, Jimmy Shott, who used to be a good foot-in-the-door reporter until he accepted a lucrative position in the advertising game. Jimmy took me to an Italian place in the West Forties, and the idea was I would meet Damon Runyon. Well, Damon did not show, but just after Jimmy and I sat down in came two prize-fight managers. One of them was an older man, around fifty, who looked not unlike an uncle of mine. His name, and also the name of my uncle, is Mike. The other manager was Hymie, and he right away began talking fighters, and was very proud of one of his boys, who had won the decision in a preliminary to the Joe Louis exhibition in which Max Baer was the third man in the ring. At one time I covered a great many fights and I long ago learned that all you have to do to get along with fight managers is to nod and keep nodding and put on a slightly sleepy look and occasionally ask either a very dumb or a very smart question (and they are interchangeable). This

54

went on while Jimmy and I ate the ravioli, and then
Jimmy interrupted Hymie and asked him to give the
wop waiter some double-talk, which isn't pig-Latin,
which isn't *anything*. Hymie smiled, very pleased, and
called the waiter. He dug his fork in a piece of veal
and turned it over and over, and said to the waiter,
"You portis on the portistan on the veal."

"Sir?" said the waiter, bowing.

"Portis. Portis on the portistan on the veal portis,
and the stamportis," said Hymie, continuing to turn
the veal over as though he had a sword with a red cape
hanging from it, like a bull-fighter.

"I don't understan', sir," said the waiter.

"God damn it! I said the portis on the portistan on
the *veal* portis and the veal—call the head waiter!"

The head waiter already was on his way, and Hymie
repeated. The head waiter shooed the waiter away and
said, "Once again will you repeat it, please?" Then
Jimmy burst out laughing and the head waiter caught
on and laughed too, but not heartily. He didn't altogether get it, because Hymie, who is thirty-five years
old, has the expression you think you see in the pictures
of cops whose widows received yesterday the Depart-
mental Medal of Honor. "Aah, what the hell," said
Hymie.

As we were getting ready to go, Hymie asked us if we would like to go to Newark to see some fights, and we said we would. He would only be a little while finishing his dinner and we waited. While we sat there smoking and drinking coffee he and I discovered that we had been in Hollywood at the same time, and of course we knew a lot of people in common. He knew bigger people than I did, and two of his pals—*but* the best—were an actor and a crooner. Every morning the crooner would call him and say: "What do you hear from the mob, Hymie?" And Hymie would reply: "The mains are coming to town. The semi-mains just took over Kansas City." And the crooner would say: "What do you hear from Louie the Lug, Hymie?" And Hymie would say: "Louie the Lug? He's from the opposition. A wrong gee, Bing. A wrong gee. Strictly an opposition guy." And then: "We're gunna straighten him out, Bing. I sent for my iron-rod gun moll, and we're gunna straighten out Louie the Lug as soon as the mains get in town. The semi-mains just took over Kansas City." This kind of conversation would go on every day, the crooner talking movie gangster slang to Hymie, and Hymie replying in kind.

Hymie finished his dinner and said good night to Mike, who was leaving, and then the three of us went

out and got in Hymie's car, being joined by Tony, a
friend of Hymie's. We drove like hell through traffic
and down the elevated highway to the entrance to the
tunnel. Hymie paid the toll, handing the Port Authority cop a dollar, and as he got his change Hymie said,
just above a whisper: "Wuddia hippum the mob?"

The cop paid no attention, and Hymie half turned
around and said to me: "An opposition guy, John.
We'll let the semi-mains take care of him. We'll get
him straightened out." By that time we had reached
the cop who takes the toll-tickets.

"Wuddia hippum the mob?" said Hymie slowly.

The cop looked at him and then at the rest of us
and said: "What mob?" but not liking it a bit.

Hymie gave the car the gas and we went down into
the tunnel.

In New Jersey our troubles began the moment we
left the Pulaski Skyway—the wrong way. We were in
Newark, but not anywhere in Newark that we wanted
to be. So every few blocks Hymie would stop and ask
for directions. We were in a tough district, but that did
not deter Hymie. After getting directions from boys
hanging around poolrooms, from motormen and cops
and women, Hymie would whisper to our informants:
"Wuddia hippum the mob?"

He always got an answer. The young men who you could tell were mob timber would say they hadn't heard anything for a couple days, or give some answer which showed they were aware that there was a mob. The motormen would just laugh and not say anything, afraid to say the wrong thing. The same with the cops, except that they did not laugh. They were simply afraid to say the wrong thing (our car was black and shiny and new). Once we encountered a wise kid who wanted to give us some repartee, and Hymie said: "Hey, *waaaaid* a minute, waid a *minute*, there, wise guy. A wronggo. An opposition guy. Maybe we better straighten 'im out."

"Hymie, we gotta get to them *fights*," said Tony.

"Yeah, but first we oughta spray this wise guy with hot lead, from our Thompson sub-machine-gun iron. This is a wise guy." But we drove on.

Hymie was in the corner for two boys or maybe three, all of them his brother's fighters, his brother also being a manager in that neck of the woods. Hymie is a good man in a corner, and I remember his boy won in one fight, another fight his boy was robbed, and I forget the other. We were sitting in the second or third row, and between rounds Hymie would talk to his boy, but just as he was climbing down from the ring he would call over to us: "Wuddia hippum the mob?" And we would point to the opposing fighter and yell out: "An opposition guy!"

"A wronggo," Hymie would say.

After the fights we went to the dressing-room while Hymie received. He also gave. He gave to the referee, who was on the take two ways. He slipped five bucks to one of the fight reporters (it is a pleasure to go out with someone like Hymie and find out which reporters, big or little, will accept cash gratuities). He picked Al Roth to beat Tony Canzoneri at the Garden (Canzoneri, of course, won). He spent a little time with the best of the boys he had seconded, trying, as he had done during the fight, to tell the boy that in a short time he would have no hands left if he persisted in punching Negroes in the head. After half an hour or so we left to continue our entertainment.

Our hosts were a handsome young man who was introduced only as Harry, and a man who looked like Warren Hymer, the movie actor, and was called Blubber. Harry told us that the week before he had organized the organ-grinders at two dollars a week per grinder. They took us to a very attractive bar and Harry called to the singer, Mabel or Melba, to come over and join us. "Sit with Hymie," said Harry. She sat next to Hymie, and he began right away:

"You uh portistan on the portis the joint?"

"Wha'?"

"Portistan. On the portis. Harry said you'd portis on the portistan the joint. That's what he told me."

"Liss-sunn," said Melba.

"Go on," said Harry. "Answer him yes or no."

"Well, if you say so," said Melba.

"I said so," said Harry.

"Well, then," said Melba.

"Oh, I don't want it that way," said Hymie. "Listen, you, Melba or whatever your name is, if you portistan the stanportis—"

"I *said* I *would*, didn't I?" she said.

"Okay, then I buy you a corsadge. You be my gun moll."

"Say, what is this?" said Melba.

"Sure. I buy you a corsadge and you put the shooting iron in it."

"Do I have to?" she asked Harry.

"What he says," said Harry.

"I tell you what I'll do for you," said Hymie. "I'll turn over my beer racket to you. I gave it to my sister but I'll take it back from her and give it to you if you'll be my gun moll. How'd you like to be my gun moll?"

"She's too dumb," said Harry. "She don't know what you're talking about. Let's eat. I want a steak. Who else wants a steak?"

The waiter came over (he didn't have to come very far) for our order, and Hymie said: "Listen, you donkey, Melba is going to be my gun moll so I want a steak, but I want a small portis with a portis on top, see? Then garnish it with a stanportis and a portis medium—"

"Medium well done, sir?" said the waiter.

"Hey, I don't even think you're listening. Now get this. A small steak with a portis, but Melba wants a portistan portis on the ubbadate stanportis *steak*, without the prawn portis. And a cup of tea, on account of Melba's going to be my gun moll, aren't you, Stupid?"

"Ha ha," she said.

"Oh, a wronggo," said Hymie.

"What's that, a wronggo?" said Harry.

"You hear him? Say, what are we, in the provinces or something? You don't know what a wronggo is? Wait till the mains hear that. The mains and the semi-mains. They just took over Bushwick from the opposition and what they're gunna do, they're gunna take over this territory next week."

"No," said Blubber.

"He's nuts," said Harry. "Don't pay no attention to him when he's like this."

"That's what I thought," said Melba.

"*Not* you," said Harry. "You're his gun moll." At that Harry burst out laughing, the only time he laughed all night.

Lunch Tuesday

IT WAS one of those good, characterless restaurants in the East Fifties, run by a former speakeasy proprietor. It was 1.25 and there was a fair-sized crowd for luncheon. Mrs. Flintridge was lighting a denicotinized cigarette—her second in twenty minutes. She was looking down at the flame when she heard a voice say, "Darling, I'm terribly sorry." Mrs. Flintridge shook the match and put it in the ashtray, heedless of the fact that the match burned on. "Have you been here long?" the newcomer asked.

"Well, I had nothing to do, so I was on time for a change," said Mrs. Flintridge.

"I'm terribly sorry, but I came in on the subway and had to stop at Macy's, and traffic really was something. What are you drinking? Is that a Daiquiri?" Mrs. Walton sat down.

"No, a Side Car," said Mrs. Flintridge.

"Oh, brandy." Then, "Are you drinking *brandy?*"

"This is my second. I got home at four this morning, or at least I think it was four. It might have been

later. We went to one of those parties at the club.
Every time we do it, either Bud or I swears we'll never
do it again during the week, but he's been pretty good
lately and I thought a little binge—"

"I'll have a Side Car, please. Two Side Cars. You're
ready for another, aren't you?"

"Oh—all right," said Mrs. Flintridge.

"Well," said Mrs. Walton, a little like a crier opening court. For the next few minutes the women talked
about traffic and shopping and what they wanted to
eat, and Mrs. Walton was persuaded to catch up with
Mrs. Flintridge's quantity of Side Cars. They thought
a little white wine with their luncheon, and then, because each had half a Side Car left, they thought no,
no wine. Mrs. Flintridge said frankly, no, she didn't
like Mrs. Walton's hat. The hat was all right, but she
thought the ribbons in the back were a little on the
long side. Mrs. Walton said that was what she was
afraid of, but she couldn't be sure. She'd have them
shortened. Maybe taken off altogether. Mrs. Flintridge said not to take them off altogether, just shorten
them. She also said she wished she could wear a hat
like that, but that Mrs. Walton didn't look thirty,
whereas she, Mrs. Flintridge, looked her thirty and
probably more. Mrs. Walton told Mrs. Flintridge

that she looked about twenty-eight, but had looked twenty-eight five years ago and would go on looking twenty-eight till after she was forty. That was better than looking younger and then all of a sudden, around thirty-two, looking older. At least that's what Mrs. Walton thought. They talked pleasantly that way, the talk of old friends who seldom saw each other any more. They came to the end of the meal and they thought a little crème de menthe, but Mrs. Walton didn't know how that would go on top of a Side Car, or a couple of Side Cars. Mrs. Flintridge said that was an exploded theory about mixing drinks. It all depended on the condition of your stomach. But of course she conceded that her own stomach wasn't in any too good condition today, what with last night, and she added, "And I'll bet Bud—"

"Well, then a brandy. A brandy'd be all right. Waiter, two brandies, please. I mean two Courvoisiers." Then, "What are your plans for this afternoon? Is there one of those Actors' Fund matinees, do you suppose? That's the trouble with Tuesday. We can't go to a matinee unless they're having one of those Actors' Fund matinees. I wish I'd have thought of it when I called you. Then we could have made it

Wednesday or Thursday. Shall I get a paper and see if there's a matinee?'"

"All right," said Mrs. Flintridge. "But it wasn't you that called me. I called *you*. You *never* call *me*."

"Oh, I *do*, Peggy, I do too. I called you the last time."

"No, I called you," said Mrs. Flintridge.

"Well, the time before."

"The time before you didn't call me. That was when Bud and I met you and Harry on the train going to New Haven."

"Oh, well, what difference does it make who calls who? Whom."

The waiter brought the newspaper, and not only was there no matinee, but the feature picture at Radio City Music Hall wouldn't be going on again till nearly four o'clock, and there was nothing else they wanted to see. Then a man came in and stood at the bar, where they could see him. He was soaking wet. His derby hat was soaking wet; his light overcoat was soaking wet; and as he spoke to the proprietor, whom he obviously knew, he was laughing in the way people do when they have been caught in a sudden downpour. "Look at that man," said Mrs. Walton. "It must be teeming.

And me with a new hat, naturally. We might as well wait here as anywhere."

"All right, let's," said Mrs. Flintridge. "I could do with another drink."

"If I have another, I'll be tight. Oh, well."

"We can ask the waiter to let us know when it stops raining," said Mrs. Flintridge. "I think I'll switch to Scotch. Brandy depresses me, and the rain." She switched to Scotch, but Mrs. Walton stuck to brandy and soda. She said, "I think I'll just have a little brandy and soda." Their drinks were brought to them and they received them in different ways: Mrs. Walton looked at hers, not touching it right away, as though it were a surprise birthday cake in a night club; and Mrs. Flintridge, the moment the waiter combined the highball, picked it up and narrowed her eyes and took a good, long drink out of it. By this time they had reached the stage where a drink could interrupt any conversation. During the silence the proprietor came over to them. *"Mesdames,"* he said, and then, addressing Peggy Walton, "Mrs. Walton, the gentleman at the bar, he asks if he may buy a drink. He sess he is a friend of Mr. Walton and has met you."

"You're being picked up. I guess the hat's all right," said Mrs. Flintridge.

"I'm sorry. I'll tell the gentleman. Please forgive me," said the proprietor.

"Oh—he looks all right," said Mrs. Walton. Somehow, in the shuffle, the man came over.

"Mrs. Walton, I didn't mean to be fresh, but I'm Arthur Luddy and I do know Harry very well, and I met you one night at the Stork Club. You were with —I forget his name."

Peggy Walton interrupted his loss of memory to introduce Mrs. Flintridge.

"Oh," said Mr. Luddy. "How do you do?" He really made it a question. He sat down and had his drink brought from the bar.

"Is the Stork Club fun?" said Mrs. Flintridge. "I've never been there, and even Bud, he's only been there once."

"I hardly ever go," said Peggy Walton. "I don't like night clubs."

"I don't as a rule, but I like the Stork," said Mr. Luddy. "You seemed to have been having a good time that night. Don't you remember at all? There's no reason why you should, but a fellow called Merle Stafford brought me over to your table to meet his partner."

"Merle Stafford?" said Mrs. Flintridge.

"Yeah. Do you know him?"

Mrs. Flintridge picked up her drink and looked down into it and slowly raised her eyes to the terrified eyes of Peggy Walton. "As a matter of fact, he's my husband's partner," said Mrs. Flintridge.

"Well, then, huh huh, I guess you know him," said Mr. Luddy, with right good humor. "I don't know him very well. I just happened to run into him, and he was a little tight, and you know—"

"Mr. Luddy," said Peggy Walton. "Do you mind if would you mind getting the hell out of here?"

"Yes, please, Mr. Luddy, will you get the hell out of here?" said Mrs. Flintridge.

"Weh-heh-hell. Notta tall. You *asked* me to sit down. Sure I'll go," said Mr. Luddy. He got up and looked from one woman to the other and went back to the bar, talking to himself. The women watched him paying his check and leaving with one more backward glance, and they watched the proprietor, who had not missed any of it, coming towards them.

"Ladies, I am very sorry. Was there something wrong?"

"It's all right. Please go away," said Mrs. Flintridge.

They looked at each other, and Peggy Walton was

suffering first of all the acute discomfort of being a little the drunker and knowing it, and wishing that of all times in her life this time she wasn't. She took a gulp of her drink and watched her hand as she put the glass down on the table.

"I tell you how it happened," she said. "Please let me. You were away somewhere and I was in town and I happened to run into Bud one afternoon. *You* know. And we—"

"Ah, what's the *use*, Peggy? I knew it was somebody. I just didn't know it was *you*, that's all."

Shave

"BUT I'D like to see you before I go back to New York," said Adams.

"Do you have to go back this afternoon?" said Morris.

"I have to be there tonight. Some time tonight."

"What time is it now?" said Morris.

Adams was holding the telephone with his left hand. He lowered the phone and looked at his wrist-watch. "Twenty after. About twenty. Eighteen. I may be a little fast."

"Well, the only trouble is—you could make it, I guess. But—do you remember how to get here?"

"I think so. Sure. It isn't hard."

"Well, if you leave right away. But I'll tell you, Johnny, if you're not here by ten of three I'll have to leave. I won't be able to wait. This is the only day they'll let me see her."

"I'll leave right away. I'll check out this minute, and I ought to be there before ten of three."

Adams got a break with the traffic lights and the cops, and he was out of Boston in good time. Although he had not been to Morris's house in more than a year, and never had been there more than three times, he began remembering landmarks, and he arrived at Morris's a few minutes ahead of time. Morris, in the same kind of Brooks suit he had worn for fifteen years, was leaning against the front door, smoking a cigarette and with one hand in his trouser pocket. He threw the cigarette away and came down the short walk to the gate, where Adams stopped the car.

"Johnny, how are you?" said Morris.

"Fine. How are you, Willie?" They shook hands across the front door of the car.

"Christ, you didn't shave! Johnny, you can't see her looking like that."

"Why, I didn't know I was going to see her. I only came out to say hello to you."

"Not at all. You mean you didn't think she was allowed to see outsiders. Well, she can. A few. Now listen, go on in and shave. I want her to see you, but not that way."

"I'm sorry. I'd have shaved if I'd known."

Adams followed Morris to the bathroom, and while he was taking off his things Morris put a new blade in the razor and held it out when Adams had finished lathering his face. Morris sat on the edge of the tub, his hat on the back of his head. He was smoking another cigarette. He watched Adams for a minute or so.

"You've put on some weight," he said.

"Look at these arms. Look at them. I'm *all* fat." Adams, not interrupting his shave, raised his elbows to indicate his arms.

"Don't you play squash or anything?"

"*Do you?*"

"No, but I don't get fat. I guess I never will. All my family, both sides were all thin people, or at least not fat." He flicked his cigarette ash on the floor. "Betsy's lost a lot of weight."

Adams did not know what to say to that. Then he said, "I hear she's a lot better."

"Where the hell'd you hear that? You didn't hear any such thing."

"Yes, I did. I heard it somewhere."

"Well, she's worse if anything. Johnny, for Christ's sake, don't you *know* about her? She'll never be any better." He flung the cigarette into the toilet. "Listen, Johnny, about this afternoon. You have to take your cue from her. When you see her, use your intelligence. If she seems all right, normal, and she wants to talk about herself, let her. Encourage her. It'll shock you, the first time you hear her saying it. 'Why, hello, Johnny,' she'll say, and then she'll say something about coming to see a nut. She always calls herself a nut. And this place she's staying at she calls her crazy-house. I asked the doctors—they have one good man there—I thought that was a hopeful sign, that she could—*you* know—talk about herself that way. Well, he's an honest guy, and said he honestly didn't think so. You remember how she used to be, she was always articulate, and for all I know *that* was part of *this*. That stuff is good for after shaving. Just use a little of it if you're not used to it, but it's pretty good. You look a hundred per cent better."

"I feel better. I did a little drinking last night." Adams put on his shirt. "Well, now do you—shall I stick around, or shall I just say hello and then leave?"

"Depends on how she is today. You see, I only see her once a week. She's allowed to go for a ride with me, not more than an hour. This week I smashed up my car. I got drunk and drove smack into the garage wall." He halted. "I might as well tell you. I had a girl with me. Christ, I have to have *some*body, don't I?"

"Was she hurt?"

"Always the practical Johnny. No, she wasn't hurt and she's a good kid. She's a little Irish girl. She knows all about Betsy."

"What does she do?"

"She's a stenographer. Secretary."

"Well, just so you don't get yourself into a jam with her. How are you and the sauce?"

"What do you mean?"

"The sauce. Drinking."

"You and your New York slang. Oh, I drink enough to keep from going stale. But I don't want you to worry about me. I'm not drinking enough to be declared incompetent. That, by the way, is the least Betsy will call herself. Incompetent. 'We incompetents,' she says. Would you like a drink now?"

"Don't you think we better get going? I've made you late enough already."

"Your watch *was* fast. We have time for one quick one," said Morris. "I think you'd better have one anyway. You may need it. And I may need it, watching you."

"Always the insulting Willie. You haven't changed at all."

"Not me," said Morris. "No-ho. Not me."

Sidesaddle

FOR PERHAPS twenty minutes the room had been all silence except for the efficient bustlings of the smiling maid and the clicks and snapping of his cigarette lighter. Then Josie's voice.

"Charles. Charl—? Oh, there you are. I was afraid you'd gone, without seeing me."

"Nope. Just getting a load of this view," he said. He turned from the window and reached out his hand.

"Aren't you going to kiss an old friend? And an old wife?" she said.

He kissed her. What the hell? The country was practically populated with men who wanted to kiss her. He kissed her again, this time full on the mouth, and he put his arms around her. She held it, or let him hold her, until an imaginary director might have called, "We'll print that."

"Sit you down," she said. "Do I look awful? Do you mind seeing me like this? You have often enough before." Her hair was tucked back over her ears, and if she had on any make-up (he suspected just a little) he was not able to tell where it began and ended.

"Well, when I knew you you didn't have—that." He nodded down at her dressing-gown, light-blue silk.

She smiled and made some sound through her nose that meant no. "Nor this," she said, indicating the Waldorf Towers; at least as much of it as they could see. "Well, that's old stuff."

"It's old stuff to *you*, Josie. They almost weren't going to let me up. I went to the desk and they gave me a card with a number on it, and I had to give it to the elevator operator. I almost went out and had a Wassermann."

"Don't say things like that, Charlie."

"Why not? That's what I felt like."

"Well, the maid," she said. "What would you like to drink?"

"Oh, I don't know. What are you drinking?"

"Nothing before seven," she said.

"What!"

"Do you *have* to say *what* that way?" she said. She gave him the well-known profile, and raised her voice slightly. "Myrtle?"

"Yes, Miss Jefferson," said the maid.

"Scotch-and-soda," said Charlie.

"Scotch-and-soda for Mr. Evans, and I think a lemonade."

"Did you just get up?" said Charlie.

"Just get up! I've been up since eight-thirty this morning. I went all the way downtown, thinking I was smart, to get my French visa, and I could have got it in Radio City."

"You could have got it through the travel agency, for that matter."

"You would tell me about that now."

"Well, honey, I didn't have much chance to tell you before. I didn't know where you were till today."

"It was in all the papers," she said. "But I don't suppose you read the movie columns. Oh, Charlie, let's not *quarrel*. I asked you to come here because I want a favor from you. That's being frank, isn't it?"

"Well, of course I knew—"

"Now, darling, don't say you knew, meaning you knew I wanted a favor or I wouldn't have called you. It's true in a way, but not the way that sounds. I mean, I feel perfectly friendly. I don't believe in being a phony after you're divorced, but I'm not as mean as it sounds, and I'm at least frank."

"All right. What is it you want? You know you'll get it, especially the way you look now. God damn it."

She smiled in acceptance of the compliment. She watched Myrtle set down the drinks, and when Myrtle had departed she leaned forward. "Charlie, have you still got that old sidesaddle?"

"What old sidesaddle?"

"That old sidesaddle of your mother's. Remember I used it the last time we went to Hartford."

"Gee, I may have," he said. "Or at least it may still be in the stable at Hartford. Why? Don't tell me you want it?"

"I do want it. That's the favor."

"That ought to be easy. That is, if it's still there, unless one of my sisters is using it. Let me think. I went home for Christmas. Nobody rode then. Last fall. Betsy. Come to think of it—I hardly ever go home, but it seems to me, I think Betsy rides side—I'm not sure—"

"Well, I am, and that's the whole point. Betsy rides sidesaddle. She rides both, but she prefers sidesaddle. I know it."

"Mm. Then it's going to be tough, or at least it may be. You know, uh—well, Betsy hasn't got money to throw around on new saddles, and—"

"And Betsy hates me. Yes, I know."

"Well, then why don't you buy one? My God, you

can have one made, to fit you. That saddle was my mother's, and I must say, much as I loved my mother—"

"Don't look at me like some assistant director. I know I can have one made. I'll have one made, for Betsy. I'll give her the price of a new one, and a bridle, or a pair of boots."

"Betsy's pretty tough," he said. "She never liked what you said about the family when—"

"Charlie, I know all about that. I'm sorry about it, and you know it was only publicity stuff. Now look here, I happen to want that saddle. *Every*body has *new* things in Hollywood. I don't like new things. At least not new saddles and things like that. Can't you get it for me, darling?"

"You know I'd like to."

"Do you want to know how much I want it? Before I left Hollywood Jack said to me, 'If you see that ex-husband of yours while you're there, I'll'—I don't know what he said. He hates you, just as much as Betsy hates me. He told me I could see anyone but you. He'd be furious, but I'm so dying to have that saddle that I had to take the chance. Please, Charlie. I'll give you the money and you can go over to that place over on Forty-sixth or wherever it is and pick out the best saddle they have, or have one made. I'll give you the money. I'll give you five hundred dollars. That ought to be enough. Then you can buy a saddle and bridle and one of those straps that goes around the horse's neck—"

"Martingale."

"—and take it up to Hartford and bring back the other one. You can be back Sunday easily."

"Betsy knows I haven't got that kind of money," he said.

"Oh, tell her some story. Tell her the man ran into you on the street and wants your business again and made you this offer. Or tell her—*I* know. Tell her somebody ordered it and then didn't call for it, so you got it cheap. Please, will you do it for me, Charlie?"

He put down his glass. "Josie, you really are a—"

She smiled. "Don't say it, darling." She put her arms around him and held him for a moment and then shut her eyes and kissed him. "Then you can bring it here Sunday night. Jack doesn't get in till Monday morning."

No Mistakes

HE CHURCH was crowded, and they were late,
and McDonald could blame no one but himself.
To begin with, he had overslept, and he no longer
could blame Jean for that. For three months now he
had taken the responsibility of their getting up in time,
and he had been very good about it until today, of all
days. Finally it was she who was awake first and had
had to rouse him. "Come on, come *on*," she had said.
"This is your party, remember." Then there were no
clean starched collars. Oh, there were plenty of winged
collars, clean as could be, lying useless in a collar box.
But no turned-down ones, and this was an occasion for
the dark-blue suit and a turned-down collar. So he had
had to go through the laundry and pick out the cleanest
of the dirty collars—one he had worn three nights ago
with a dinner jacket. It wasn't too clean, either, but it
was the best there was. Then the taxi-driver never had
heard of Shakespeare Avenue. He was a Brooklyn taxi-
driver, and McDonald was not too sure himself how
to get to Shakespeare Avenue. They got there, and the

church was crowded, Mass had begun, and they had to kneel in the aisle.

McDonald got up and went to the usher. "Listen, I have an invitation—"

"I can't help that," the usher said. "You see what it says: 'Kindly be in your pew fifteen minutes before Holy Mass begins.'"

"I know, but we came all the way from Nineteenth Street, and my wife can't kneel on that hard floor."

"Sh-h-h. Other people are kneeling."

"But she's pregnant. She shouldn't kneel at all. Anyway, she's a Protestant."

That was what made the difference. "Well, I'll see if I can get somebody to move over. You won't get two together, though."

"That's all right. Just so she won't have to kneel. Thanks," said McDonald.

"I'll see what I can do." The usher walked down the aisle slowly, counting the people in the pews on the Epistle side, and then returning, counting the people in the pews on the Gospel side. Halfway down he stopped at a pew and leaned over to the man at the first seat. Apparently he knew the man, because he smiled and the man smiled and nodded vigorously, and the usher came back and told McDonald he had a seat for Jean.

"You go ahead," McDonald said.

"But—I don't know when to stand up and everything."

"Just watch the others. Anyway, just sit," he said. "I'll be right here. Go on."

She went to the pew, accompanied by the usher. The usher's friend, holding his hat in one hand and a string of rosary beads in the other, got up and stood in the aisle, and Jean entered and the man followed her in. It was a tight fit, and McDonald saw Jean being glared at by the hard-faced Irishwoman on her left. The usher came back and McDonald thanked him again, and at last was able to watch O'Connor.

Naturally he expected Gerald O'Connor to do everything according to the rubrics, even though it was O'Connor's first High Mass. Still, even though McDonald expected it, he was glad to see that Okie made no mistakes. McDonald told himself that even he, after all these years, probably could fake a Mass. As an altar boy he had served probably hundreds of them. Even now he remembered practically all of the Latin responses—even the Suscipiat and the Confiteor. The Suscipiat, although shorter, was harder, for some reason. The Confiteor—all you had to do was memorize the first half, up to ". . . *mea culpa, mea culpa, mea maxima culpa,*" and then you went into "*Ideo precor,*" and changed the case endings of the first half. Something like that. It was like swimming or riding a bicycle, or more like shorthand. Once you learned it, you never completely forgot it. Still, even though Okie had been studying it every day for ten years, it was nice to see he didn't get rattled and go to the wrong place or get in the way of the deacon or the subdeacon. The old priest, who wore the dalmatic of the deacon—he probably was the pastor of this church. The young guy, the subdeacon—he probably was some classmate of Okie's from the seminary.

All the new friends Okie must have, and yet Okie had remembered to send him an invitation. McDonald wondered just how much or how little Okie knew about him. He had not written to Okie for five years or more; much more. More like eight years. And he had not seen him since the year Okie had entered the seminary. Yet Okie surely must have found out by this time that he had married out of the Church and was living in New York. The invitation had been sent to the McDonald home in Waterbury, and, like all such mail, it had been forwarded to the office.

He listened to Okie, who had a deep voice, softly, weakly singing "Glo-o-oria in excelsis De-e-o." He watched him coming down from the altar. His vestments didn't seem to fit him. The—what was it?—the amice almost looked like a scarf, and was no whiter than Okie's face. The chasuble *was* too big for him, and at the bottom step the alb got in his way and he half tripped. It seemed strange to see that old priest, the deacon, formally assisting Okie, a big young man who had been called a tower of strength against Colgate, Harvard, and Boston College. McDonald wondered what Jean was thinking of it all. He was afraid he knew what she was thinking. In her church a man who wore a tie and a business suit would get up and read, and then preach, and hymns would be sung in English. . . . Yes, he was afraid he knew what Jean was thinking.

The Mass went on, and presently it was very quiet and the quiet was not really broken by the bells, and McDonald bowed his head but did not lower his eyes. He wanted to watch Jean, he wanted to be with her, to touch her hand. She turned around and smiled, and he smiled at her.

Then after a long while the Mass was over and people began to go, and Jean got up and joined him. She took his arm, and they did not say anything until they were out of the church.

He couldn't help feeling the way he did; the whole thing was exhilarating. But he didn't have to say so. "We can get a taxi at the corner and go to Okie's house. We won't have to stay long, but I want you to meet him."

"All right. What was it when everybody got very quiet and O'Connor leaned over and sort of kissed the altar? Only he didn't kiss it."

"When the bells rang?"

"Yes."

"The bells rang three times, and then a minute later three times again?"

"Yes."

"That was the Consecration."

"Oh, *that* was the Consecration. I liked that part. I liked some of the singing, but I guess I'd have liked it better if I knew Latin."

He laughed. "How many people there do you think know Latin?"

"Well," she said, "I was wondering. There were quite a few that didn't look as though they knew English, let alone Latin. There was a terrible woman sitting next to me. She kept pushing me all through the service, except for that one part."

In the taxi he held her hand. It was not far to Okie's house. A butler, probably hired for the occasion, opened the door, and a huge gray-haired man in a cutaway greeted them. He said he was Dr. O'Connor, Gerald's father, and this was Gerald's mother—Mr. and Mrs. McDonald. Oh, yes. Mac. Gerald's roommate in college. Well, well—and McDonald was fairly sure that the Doctor took a professional look at Jean. Well, well. Gerald would be down right away. Meanwhile, a little champagne never hurt anybody, and they had champagne, and a well-dressed girl, thirty or so, introduced herself. Okie's sister. And introduced other people to the McDonalds, Gerald's roommate at college and his wife. Well, well. I'll bet you're proud of Gerald today. His roommate. He'll make a fine priest. And another man in a cutaway, a lawyer, a man about thirty-five, whom people called Counselor. Okie's brother. "I thought I recognized you from the Stork Club," said this O'Connor. And a lot of old ladies, who Never Touched It. "Neither touch, taste, nor handle," he heard two of them say.

"He'll be here in a minute. I hope," said McDonald. "Let's sit down over here."

He took Jean to a chair, which everyone was politely leaving vacant for everyone else. Then after a few minutes Okie appeared, beaming over his Roman collar.

"He looks like Spencer Tracy," said Jean.

"You're crazy," said her husband.

"Well, reminds me of him. In that earthquake picture."

" 'San Francisco.' But you're crazy. He looks about as much like Spencer Tracy as I do."

There was no use getting up. Okie had a lot of blessings to give. One or two of the old ladies, apparently anticipating the time when Okie would have the ring of a bishop, kissed his hand. The old ladies, and the young ladies, and the men and the children, they all would ask Father O'Connor for his blessing, and McDonald could read Okie's lips saying, "Be glad to," and they would kneel and Okie would mumble, very fast, the blessing, and so on he moved until he saw McDonald. At that moment someone was asking for his blessing, but he hurried to McDonald.

"Mac! You old rat. How are you? Were you at the Mass?"

"I sure was. Okie, I want you to meet my wife. Jean, this is Father O'Connor."

"How are you, Jean?"

"How do you do, Father?"

"When did all this happen, Mac? And why didn't I get an invitation?"

"Well," said McDonald. "There weren't any. We, uh—"

"Waterbury girl?" said Okie.

"No. New York."

"You should have waited—when'd you say you were married?"

"About six months ago," said McDonald.

"Ah, you should have waited. Then I could have married you," said Father O'Connor, looking at Jean. "Or *could* I?"

"No, I guess you couldn't, Okie," said McDonald.

"I see," said the priest. Then, "Well, it was nice of you to come. Help yourself to some champagne."

A woman tugged at his cuff. "Father, can I have your blessing? I remember when you used to—"

"Glad to," said O'Connor. "Excuse me," he said to the McDonalds.

McDonald sat beside his wife and they watched Okie moving around to the other side of the room, and when he had reached the farthest corner Jean spoke. "Go?" she said.

"Yes, I guess so," said McDonald.

Brother

THERE were a lot of voices; there was one author-ized voice singing "I'm Putting All My Eggs in One Bas-ket"; there was a fine jazz orchestra wasting its arrangements on three hundred and fifty unheeding persons; seltzer bottles squawked their bottom drops into highball glasses. At the moment there was no con-versation at one table, around which were seated four persons, three ugly men and a pretty girl. The girl was sitting so she could see the dancers, and the men were characteristically looking over their shoulders at the dancers, at people at other tables, at people entering the place. This was Hollywood.

"Hello."

The four persons glanced at one tall, thin young man, pale of face, blond of hair, and garbed in a gun-club-check jacket and dark-blue flannel slacks. Around his neck a silk scarf.

"Hello, Leonard," said the pretty girl.

"Can I sit down with you?" said Leonard.

"Sit down," said one of the men.

"How's Ruthie?" said the pretty girl.

"Fine," said Leonard.

"Yeah, how's Ruthie?" said one of the men.

"She's fine," said Leonard.

"How's your mother?" said another of the men.

"Fine. I just left her," said Leonard.

"Have a drink, Leonard?" said the third man.

"I'll have a beer," said Leonard. "I'll pay for it, though."

"Naah," said the first man. "Waiter, give him a beer."

"I'm only drinking beer," said Leonard.

"Fattening," said one of the men.

"He can use it," said another.

"Yes," said Leonard. "I want to put on some weight."

"Where's Ruthie tonight?" said a man.

"I don't know. I thought she'd be here."

"That's for me, that Ruthie," said another man.

"Yeah, I go for that. I'm glad she's not my sister." They all laughed.

"I bet Leonard's glad she's *his* sister," said a man. The men laughed.

"Shut up, wise guy," said the pretty girl. "All of you."

"They can't kid me," said Leonard. "I got plenty of that even before I came out here. Where I used to work they'd always try to kid me about me being Ruthie's brother. They used to call me that, Mr. Ruth Rugby."

"Where'd she ever get that name, Rugby?"

"Rogowicz," said Leonard. "Rugby is a school in England, also a game."

"I heard of the game," said a man.

"Well, what's with you, Leonard?"

"How do you mean, what's with me?" said Leonard.

"You gettin' much?"

"Oh, shut up, you guys," said the pretty girl. "Leonard's a nice kid. Leave him alone."

"Oh, they can't kid me," said Leonard. "I got a letter from a friend of mine back in New York Monday. He said I suppose you're right in there with those chorus girls for Ruthie's next picture. I wouldn't do that. Wouldn't that be a smart thing if Ruthie's brother got mixed up with some chorine?"

"Chorine, is it?" said a man. "Say. The gaberoo."

"He knows from nothin'," said another man.

"Don't pay any attention to them, Leonard. Did they start shooting yet on Ruthie's new picture?"

"Yes. Yesterday. I'm glad," said Leonard.

"What the hell, she gets paid anyway," said a man.

"I'll slap your face, Louis Harrow," said the pretty girl. "Why are you glad, Leonard?"

"Oh, gives me more to do. I get tired of doing nothing. When she's working at the studio I drive her to work every morning. I do it for something to do."

"Why don't you go to college? U.C.L.A. *That's* a big college," said the girl.

"Well, I don't know. I never finished high school," said Leonard.

"They hadda burn down the school to get him outa the freshman class," said a man.

"Oh, geezes. With Cantor they'll have you next," said another.

"Why don't you go home, wise guy?" said the girl.

"Some people haven't got anything else to do but make cracks. Agents," said Leonard.

"Who ast you to sit here if you don't like it?" said the man.

"Parasites that live on their ten per cent that they didn't earn," said Leonard.

"Don't answer him, Leonard. Don't give him that much satisfaction," said the pretty girl.

"Go out and call up Ruthie," said another man.

"I would, only I don't know where she is," said Leonard.

"I could tell you," said another man.

The others snickered.

"You only think you could," said Leonard. "I went by there and her car isn't there."

"Oh, he knows," said a man.

"Dirty, evil-minded bastards, all of you," said the pretty girl. "Don't mind them, Leonard."

"Certain people try to get somewhere and they don't, so they get sore. You know, Peggy," said Leonard.

"She knows, all right," said a man. "Nobody's sore at Peggy."

"Wade a minute," said another man.

"Oh, all right," said the man who had made the crack.

"Well," said the man who had resented the crack.

"Of course it's all right what she calls me because I want to rib this punk. Sure. I'm a bastard because I rib Leonard."

"He's right," said Peggy's defender. "You oughtn't of called him that."

"Then what right does he have to say things like that about Leonard's sister?" said Peggy.

"It ain't for you to insult your friends, though. Nobody ast Leonard to come to this table. Not even you.

So don't call your friends names like that. I don't like it. You owe Louis an apology."

"I'll owe it to him," said Peggy. "I guess you better go sit with some other people, Leonard."

"I was just going to," said Leonard. "Good night, Peggy."

"Good night, Leonard," said Peggy.

"Gi' my regards to Ruthie," said a man.

"She wouldn't even know your name," said Leonard, going.

"That's what *you* think," said the man. "I have a notion to give him a punch in the nose. Punk."

They watched Leonard. A few people spoke to him, with that expression in which there is full recognition, achieved without a nod and with only an almost imperceptible movement of the lips. It so uncompromisingly means, Don't sit down. Then he was gone out of sight.

Saffercisco

WHILE Jack Grant is not the world's most famous movie actor, it can be truthfully said that he has been; and even today his name on the marquee of the Paramount in Palm Beach or the Majestic in Tamaqua, Pa., means box office. But it is not with his power as a draw that this little anecdote is concerned. Maybe it would be better to say that among his four or five wives (many persons are vague as to whether he ever actually was married to one of the ladies) are two of the, say, fifteen most popular movie actresses. And among those fifteen at least two more have been his mistress. That score more or less establishes the fact that Jack got around, and when he fell for Maude Hislip it was as much of a surprise to him as it was to anyone.

She came out to Hollywood on the crest. That is, she had been in one hit, one forced-run play, and several turkeys. Shortly after she came to Hollywood, she married Bobby Waterman, the writer. (He is the kind of writer whose name is inevitably followed by the appositional "the writer.") They got veiled up and were together about two years when Jack met Maudie.

Well, he fell in love. He had met her at parties, but then suddenly one day he really saw her, and loved her dearly. He also liked Bobby Waterman. Jack thought it over and thought it over and talked with a friend (an old girl friend) about it, and he made up his mind that he had to marry Maudie. So he called her up and asked her if he might come to dinner the following Friday, and Maudie said she'd be delighted. What Jack wanted to do was to lay his cards on the table; say to Bobby, "Bobby, I love Maudie and I want to marry her." Open and aboveboard. Honest. Decent. Civilized. He could hardly wait till Friday. He consulted his old girl friend about what clothes to wear: whether to wear the tweed jacket and flannel slacks, or dinner coat, or tails. The girl friend said he would be wise to wear tails; it was a momentous occasion, and besides he was at his handsomest in tails.

So that Friday Jack was dressed and ready at seven, and he had a couple of drinks and drove out to Santa Monica, arriving at Maudie and Bob's around eight o'clock. Bob was in riding breeches and coat, with a scarf around his neck, and he greeted Jack pleasurably and obviously sincerely. They had a drink together and a few more, and no sign of Maudie, but Jack didn't want to be hasty or gauche or anything like that, so he did not say anything. They had a lot of drinks, fast, and nine o'clock came and no sign of Maudie and no sign of dinner. And they were getting stewed. Jack read a lot, and they covered the world's literature, then they talked movie politics and exchanged funny stories about producers and things that had happened to them on location and all about horses and dogs, and Jack thought he never had met a more charming guy, and Bobby not only thought so, but in time came to the point of telling Jack so. "I didn't know you were such a nice guy," Bobby said. "You know, I *like* you. I thought you were more or less of a heel at first, but you're all right. O.K. You ought to do this oftener— drop in for dinner."

"Drop in?" said Jack. "I didn't drop in. Wuddia mean drop in? Maude knew I was coming."

"Did she? Didn't say anything to me about it. Oh, well, I don't care. Here you are, so let's have a powder, one more little powder, then we'll go in and graze. Wunnia say?"

"Sure, but what about Maude? Don't you think we oughta wait for Maudie?"

"Oh." Bobby began to laugh quietly. He looked

down into his drink and shook his head, signifying nothing. He kept it up until he exasperated Jack.

"What is this?" said Jack. "Didn't Maudie expect me?"

"Don't think so. If she did, she didn't tell me, Jack." Bobby cleared his throat and changed his tone. "You know where she is, don't you? You don't mean to tell me that you don't *know* where Maudie *went*. Don't you know where Maudie is?"

"No, of course I don't. I had a dinner engagement right here in this house. Right *here*." He made a gesture like an umpire indicating Strike One. "Where is she?"

"Saffercisco."

"Sa' Fra'cisco?"

"S-a-n Fran-*cis*co."

"You mean on location, or what? A personal appearance?"

"No, no. No, no, no, no, no. Maudie is up in Saffercisco spending the weekend with Harry Lotterman, her director."

"What do you mean?" said Jack.

"What do you mean, what do I mean? You know what I mean. She went away with Harry Lotterman for the weekend. Wunnia think I mean? Jack, you're not dumb. You're a big boy now. Wunnia mean, what do I mean? What kinda talk is that, Jack?"

"You mean to sit here and tell me your wife goes to Sa' Fra'cisco with a louse like that and you just sit here?"

Bobby looked at him a long time, wet his lips a couple of times, getting ready to talk, and then he gazed at his cigarette until he began to get cross-eyed. Then he said, "Well, Jack, I'll tell you. I wanna tell you something. Listen to me, Jack, while I tell you this. Maudie, the first time she did this I just coudn't stand it. It hurt me. It hurt me, Jack. And then the second time. That hurt me, too. Really did. Bu-u-ut then, you know you can only stand so much, Jack. Only so much. Then you begin to get used to it. I had to get used to it, Jack. And let me tell you something"—he leaned over and tapped Jack's knee—"Jack, old boy, you might as well get used to it, too."

Ice Cream

PEOPLE standing in front of shops and hotels watched with dull, exhausted interest Harry's progress up the street. They gave him about the same perfunctory attention that their ears gave to the elevated trains half a block away on Sixth Avenue. Harry was carrying something in a paper bag, holding the bag in front of him and walking as fast as he could, in short, quick steps. It was just too awful that anybody should be in such a hurry on a night as hot as this. There were blots of perspiration on his light-blue "polo" shirt, but he looked cool—or at least not hot. His shirt was open at the neck and had half-sleeves. He wore suspenders and he had on a wrist-watch that had square metal links instead of a strap.

He turned in at one of the hotels and went up a flight of stairs to a street-front room. Inside lay a big mound of a woman, on the bed. Her face was made up, even to the blue eye-shadow; but her lip rouge, obviously put on in the same style she had used when her face was much smaller, did not make her face look

smaller now. Her fingers and breasts were small, but
the flesh rolled down on the backs of her hands and
over her ankles, and under the black net négligé she
was huge in the hips and abdomen and thighs. She was
smoking a cigarette, and two independent curls of smoke
came out of her nostrils and hung in the air in front
of her face. She waved the smoke away as Harry came
in.

"No more strawberry," he said. "They ran out of it,
so I got burnt almond."

"Burnt almond! Burnt—almond! Why didn't you
get plain vanilla, then? Burnt almond!"

"All right," said Harry. "Just eat the chocolate,
then, if you don't want the burnt almond. I wasn't
going to call you up and waste a nickel at the drug-
store to find out what kind of ice cream you wanted."

"You could of thought a minute, and if you had any
sense you'd of remembered about my cavity. I can't eat
burnt almond with this cavity. It has nuts in it, you
dope."

"Yah. You and your cavity. I don't see why you
don't go and have it filled. It sure would be worth it
to me if you'd get it filled. What would you do if you
were going to have a kid, if you're that afraid of a
little thing like going to the dentist? My God!" He

dished out some ice cream, putting half in one saucer, half in another.

"No fears," she said. "Anyway, who ever heard of going to the dentist for a baby? I'm sure I didn't. What's the dentist got to do with that, I'd like to ask?"

"Either you're pretty dumb or else is this your idea of a gag, because if it's your idea of a gag, you're my idea of dumb. Not that you ain't anyway."

"Oh, skip it. Skip it, and pass me the stuff. You took long enough getting it, till I thought there for a minute I better send little Oscar out to look for you and see if he could find you, didn't I, Oscar-Woscar?" A little dog on the floor held up its head and then lowered it again.

"Well," said Harry, sitting down to his share of the ice cream, "I was delayed on account of I happened to run into a friend of yours over near the B.-M.T. entrance."

"Who?" she said.

"Wuddia mean, who? You don't have that many friends that you can't guess who."

"Oh, come on. Not in this heat. Who did you see, a friend of mine?"

"Well, if you must know, it was—oh, I don't know if I ought to tell you. I might enkindle the light of love all over again." He put a heaping spoonful of ice cream in his mouth and drew the spoon out slowly, leveling it off.

"What do you mean by that, may I ask? You mean you saw some beautiful doll, I guess. Some beautiful little doll from Shreveport, Louisiana, that had a father that owned a bank, and she wanted you to run away with her when you were with Whiteman. Don't give me that again, for God's sake."

"Did I say anything about a doll? Did I? I said a friend of yours, didn't I? I didn't say anything about any friend of mine. This one's no friend of mine, the party I saw."

"Well, then, for the sixtieth time, who was it?"

"It was none other than Lank Long."

"Lank! My husband? Where'd you see him? Are you—what are you giving me, Harry? Is this a rib, or what?"

"I'm only trying to tell you. I ran into Lank Long. Your first husband, by the way. Not your husband. You're married to me now. Remember? Remember marrying me? Anyway, I was coming out of the drug-store and I saw this piece of humanity standing near the B.-M.T. entrance. He had a fiddle under his arm, but that didn't make me think anything. You never can tell who's going to turn out to be a fiddle-player, so I was getting ready to walk by him when he turned and recognized me. We said hello, me very you-know, giving him the cold eye and so on, and right off the reel he asked about you—"

"Wud he have to say about me?"

"—and he said he heard I married you and I said yes, and to change the subject I asked him what he was doing and he said he was kind of waiting around, hoping to see Tommy or Jimmy Corsey, I forget which he said, and I didn't pay much attention. He's such a liar, and in addition to that I wasn't innarested in his doings, but only to make conversation I asked him that question. Well, he said he was going to make a record with a couple of the boys, and I said that's funny, I thought they would be using Benuti if they were looking for a fiddle-player. Naw, he said. Not Benuti, he said. Benuti's all washed up, he said. No good any more. 'Is that so?' I said. I said I seemed to hear Benuti was doing all right, but Mr. Long said no, Benuti was all washed up."

"Then what? How did he look?"

"Looked all right. Looked in the money, in fact, and I guessed he noticed me sizing him up and studying him, because right away he explained how he happened to have this swell outfit. He had a pair of sport shoes and tan coat and flannel trousers, like I had when I was with Lopez, and so your Mr. Long said he happened to have the outfit from when he was working with Fiorito out in Chicago. Fiorito out in Chicago, for God's sake! Telling me where Fiorito is. Me, one of Ted's best friends. He has the nerve to tell me whereabouts Fiorito is and gives me this about getting an outfit working with Ted, when I know Ted wouldn't give him work without me hearing about it. Well, I guess he could see I was thinking, because that was when he had the nerve to try and put the touch on me."

"Asked you for money?"

"Asked me for money is right. He saw me looking him over, and then he said, 'Harry, I'll come clean with you. Right now,' he said, 'I'm on the nut. I need a five-dollar bill, because when I meet these fellows I want to take them over to the Onyx and buy them anyway a round of drinks.' Yeah, I thought. And what about the tab you owe at the Onyx? He owes plenty there for over a year. So I let him have it, plenty. 'Listen here, you heel,' I said. 'If you're trying to put the arm on me for dough just because I happen to have taken your wife away from you when you weren't *man* enough to hold her, if that's what you have in mind, you better forget it,' I said, 'because when Betty gave you the air and came and lived with me, did I bother to collect the thirty-seven bucks you owed me?' I said. I said, 'Now you're back in town, I think what I'll do is get a judgment out against you for that thirty-seven bucks. I can use thirty-seven bucks, and as for lending you any more—huh,' I said."

"What did he say to that? Was he sore when you said it about how I gave him up for you? I bet that burned him up."

"Well, I suppose it did, but he couldn't let on, because he was trying to make a touch. Anyway, I knew all the time he didn't have any dough, and that about getting a judgment out against him, how could I? I have nothing to prove he owes me a nickel. But of course he's too stupid to figure that out. So he said all he had was a few clothes and his fiddle. If that's the same fiddle he used to have, I told him, why, Bob Motherwell would be willing to give him a hundred-dollar note for it. I said, 'Go sell the fiddle to Bob and pay me what you owe me. But if you don't get it up, cash on the line, inside of twenty-four hours, I'll get a judgment and take the fiddle away and sell it myself.' Well, did he crawfish on that! Sure, he'd positively have the money for me. Where could he get in touch with Bob? Where was I staying? So forth and so on."

"Then what?"

"Then I walked away. But I guess that's the last I'll hear of Mr. Long, the maestro. Either he'll sell Bob the fiddle and beat it out of town, or else beat it without selling the fiddle and try to get a job with some band on the road. And you know what chance of getting a job on the road anybody has. But I got rid of him."

"He's getting what he deserves. But imagine all the dough he used to have, and now he hasn't even the price of a meal, most likely. He used to have a La Salle automobile, and a trunkful of clothes to wear and all the money a person would need, and now the poor dope —starving for lack of food."

"What the hell? Who wants to eat in this weather?"

"Who wants to eat? Maybe you don't," she said, "but you ought to see the justice I could do to some more of that ice cream. But not that burnt almond."

Peggy

Aren't they sweet together, those two? Look at them. *Look.* Did you see? He just kissed her on the ear, right out in front of everybody. Now, I don't care what you say, those two. If I ever saw two people. You know, it makes me want to get up and give them a push and say, "Go on, go on, you two. Get married and be happy." It really does. They're made for each other. You know, they come here for dinner every night, or at least every night I've been here this year. Every single time I've been here for dinner, here they were. And always like this. Now watch them when they dance. They're getting up to dance. You're sitting in a bad place to see them at the table, but now you'll be able to see them.

She's good, isn't she? She used to dance profession- ally, you know. . . . Oh, yes. When she first came back from Hollywood—they were stinking to her out there. She came back, and right away—John Powers. She had this money, of course, but as she said to me, "If I can possibly help it, I'm going to touch as little of that money as I possibly can." I guess she thought everybody *knew* about it, but only the Coast crowd and a few here in New York. I happened to know about it, but a lot of people didn't, and I admired her. She had enough so she could—you know, travel. She didn't have to work, but right away she got this job modeling for John Powers. She got lots of work, because she's got that kind of figure, and her face, it's that sort of not-quite-homely that's rather cute. It gets them. I've seen her at parties with the absolutely prettiest girls in New York. I remember a pary at the Casino several years ago—Brownie and that crowd gave it—and I swear to you, and nothing against *her*, far from it, she was the unprettiest girl at the party. But oh-ho-ho! All these men, artists, accustomed to seeing the real so-called beauties, they flocked around her like—anything. And the other girls were *fu*rious! Livid! That's the trouble. She isn't really popular with most of the girls, and I don't think it's fair, because she has a lot of likeable qualities, but you know how girls are. How many popular girls with men are really sincerely liked by other women?

That, of course, that's what happened in Hollywood. She went out there from some night club in, I think, Chicago. Sigmund Bernette was in Chicago; I think it

was for some kind of a Legion of Decency convention
about two years ago. I *know* that, because I was with
Bernette then, and I remember—oh, God, what a time.
I was sort of in charge of fashion stills for the magazines in the East, and we got this memo saying the heat
was on and lay off sexy pictures of our stars. Then
Bernette went to Chicago and gave the speech of his
life, telling how Bernette Pictures would co-operate to
the fullest degree, and any suggestions, et cetera. You
may not believe it just to look at Bernette, but when he
gets up there.

So of course he went to this night club where she was
dancing, and to make a long story short, inside of a
week little Peggy was on the Chief. Well, he signed
her up to a long-term contract, but without options. I
think three years, at seven-fifty a week. Well, of course
that wasn't known right away. She had an agent, and
the agent would pick up her check every week. But
she not only didn't get in any picture, but there was no
publicity on her. She wasn't even announced for a picture. What a life! Beautifully dressed and, as I say,
quite attractive. She'd go to the Vendome one day and
the Derby the next, and then the Vendome and then
the Derby. Always got a good table. But always with
the same two or three girls, and never any men. Oh,

Bernette. He's too smart for that. I've seen Bernette go into the Vendome while she was there and bow to the girl with her and pretend he didn't even know Peggy. In fact, I'm pretty sure I saw him being introduced to her a couple of times. A lot of men of course tried to move in, but I will say for Peggy, she handled them beautifully. That's another thing about Bernette. He doesn't trust anybody. For a while he'd let her go out with this little pansy in the music department. He was a beautiful dancer. But one night Bernette happened to get a load of Peggy doing a rumba with Jackie, and from then on. See what I mean? Isn't she marvelous? She's really primitive.

Well, that was her life. Car, clothes, money—and nothing to do but be there for Bernette. Then she took sick and he sent her to the desert, and of course the doctor had to be one of those handsome young California Nordics. Bernette was *fu*rious! Livid. But there wasn't much he could do, in a way. I mean, she had this wonderful contract and—oh, perhaps two years to run. So what he did, he got to her agent and told him, he said sure, he knew the contract would be tough to break in a court of law, but he told this agent, he said, "You have a lot of other clients, and I imagine some of them would like to work on this lot, but if you're going to be tough about Peggy's contract, you might just as well forget there is any such studio as the Bernette." So of course the agent hemmed and hawed, and the result was Peggy settled for one year's salary in cash. And the ironic thing was I heard several times how smart Bernette was in getting rid of deadwood, settling contracts with people that were drawing salary but not doing anything.

So she came back with this money, and I admire her; she went right to work, and in no time this young Williamson is carrying the torch, and I hear when he's twenty-five, he comes into something like four million dollars from his grandmother. Of course he hasn't a brain in his head, but he *is* nice-looking, and I imagine —well, Peggy's no gold-digger or she could have made it unpleasant for Mr. Bernette, but then what if she had and there'd had been all that publicity? Williamson would have known all about it, instead of which all he knows is he has a very attractive girl, who makes a good living with a respectable job, and is good fun and doesn't try to take him for any money. Get the check and we'll stop and say hello to them on the way out. I'd just like to hear what on earth they talk about.

And You Want a Mountain

THE MAN on the high, leather-padded stool in the office of the Schwartz Garage began to speak, and if you had been on the other side of the garage window you might have thought he was speaking to the ledger on the desk in front of him.

"I notice somebody didn't have to work late last night after all," he said.

"I beg your pardon, Mr. Loughran." The girl turned the wheel on the small adding machine and tore off a strip of paper.

"I said I notice somebody didn't have to work late last night after all," said Mr. Loughran.

"No. Mr. Schwartz said I didn't have to. I got out about six."

"A little before," said Mr. Loughran.

"Oh, spying."

"Not spying, Miss J. That's an unfair accusation."

"You call it an unfair accusation, I call it spying. Let's call the whole thing off."

"You are being unfair, Miss J. If you recall, I said

to you yesterday afternoon, it was right after when the fellow was here from the jobber, and when he left I said to you, 'Miss J, I have a ride home with a friend of mine that has a car if you'd care to go with me, or rather us.' Those were my words verbatim. Agreed?"

"Yes."

"Well then, I told you as early as three o'clock yesterday afternoon I said a friend of mine was stopping for me, so if he was late and if I was still around to see you didn't have to work after hours, is that my fault? At least give me credit for not spying on anyone. I don't spy on *any*one, Miss J. Those are tactics beneath my consideration. I don't mind being accused of something if I'm guilty, but when I'm not guilty and some person accuses me of something then I don't like it. You'd think we've known each other long enough so you wouldn't accuse me of a thing like that. You've been here two years now, Miss J, and in all that time I have never given you any reason to accuse me of those tactics. That's all I have to say."

"I apologize."

"No need to apologize. You were firmly convinced that I was spying, so it's a little too soon for you to have a change of heart. What's the matter with me, Miss J?"

"What do you mean what's the matter with you?"

"What I say. What's the matter with me? I don't know how many times in the last two years I've offered to do little things for you and you refuse as if I'd made you a proposition."

"Oh, I don't."

"Yes, you do. Several times when this friend of mine has stopped for me I've asked you if you cared for a lift, instead of riding home in the subway. Most people would jump at the chance. I know I do. I'd rather have a breath of fresh air and get home a few minutes late than ride in the subway, any day. But every time I asked you you'd think I was a White Slaver."

"Oh, I do not," said Miss J. "You know, Mr. Loughran, you're making a mountain out of a mole-hill."

"Yes, that's the trouble," said Mr. Loughran. "It's because I'm a molehill and you want a mountain."

"I don't follow."

"It's simple. My size. Because of my stature. Naturally I know how tall I am, or rather how tall I'm not, and I also see you going home occasionally with the fellows that call for you, and they're all tall, whereas I'm under average heightth."

"Why, I never gave that a thought."

"Didn't you? Well, that makes it worse if you didn't. Just because Nature didn't see fit to give me heightth, people think of me as if I were some kind of a freak or something. Not that I'm as short as all that. I'm tall enough to be in the National Guard. But of course no Johnny Weissmuller or one of those. Well, it isn't size that counts, Miss J. All you have to do is take a look at our payroll and see that. Who's the biggest employee we have on our payroll, outside of the colored fellow Cole?"

"Grady."

"Right. And what does Grady get?"

"Twenty-two fifty."

"Right. And who is the shortest one on our payroll?"

"Well, I guess you and Harry."

"Right. Harry's even a little shorter than me, if you want to be exact. And I don't have to stretch my neck to look up at Mr. Schwartz himself, either, for that matter. There isn't more than an inch between us."

"Are you inferring that if you're tall you're dumb? Because I'm considered tall for a girl, Mr. Loughran."

"I wasn't inferring anything at all, Miss J, and anyway I keep the female sex out of this discussion. All I infer is this, your brains aren't in your legs."

"I beg your pardon."

"A *man's* legs. You don't have to be tall to have brains, and it's brains that count. They pay off on brains, as they say. Look at that picture, 'Snow White and the Seven Little Dwarfs.' Walter Disney. I never met him personally, and he isn't any giant. But he's a regular genius. He'll make millions out of that picture. Millions. Take the most famous lover of our time, King Edward, the one that married Mrs. Simpson, threw away his crown to marry the woman he loves. Is he a Johnny Weissmuller? He is not."

"What have you got against Johnny Weissmuller, Mr. Loughran?"

"Johnny Weissmuller? Me? Nothing. Nothing personal. I never met the gentleman. For all I know he might be a very charming fellow. Not much of an actor, though. I just happen to mention him because he's tall."

"He makes five thousand a week."

"Oh, now listen. Five thousand a week? Two thousand maybe, but not five thousand."

"All right. I'll settle for two thousand and Johnny Weissmuller."

"You're kidding. He'd drive you crazy of boredom. I never met the gentleman, but I bet inside of two weeks he'd drive you crazy—"

"Before that."

"Exactly. Then what would you want to marry him for?"

"Who said anything about marrying him? I'm sure I didn't."

"You inferred it. You said you'd take two thousand a week and Johnny Weissmuller."

"I sure would," said Miss J. "I'd take two thousand without Johnny. Or Johnny without the two thousand."

"Oh, you have a yen for Johnny? Is that what you mean?"

"You catch on very quickly, Mr. Loughran."

"I never would have believed it. I thought you were more the mental type."

"I can be mental if I have to, Mr. Loughran, but that isn't all there is to life, if you get what I mean."

"I suppose you could go for Grady."

"Grady's all right. I saw Grady lift up the hind end of a Fordor coop."

"Yes, but meanwhile all he lifts out of this company

is twenty-two fifty a week. You couldn't live on that."

"Who said anything about living on it, and anyway I could live on it. I live on less. But who said anything about living on it. Just because a man has a handsome physique doesn't mean I want to marry him and live on his twenty-two fifty a week, does it? Or am *I* wrong?"

Mr. Loughran slid down off his stool, work sheet in hand, and faced Miss J. "You don't realize what you're saying," he said, and went out, slamming the frail door of the little office.

"Oh, don't I?" said Miss J.

Pal Joey

DEAR PAL TED:

Well at last I am getting around to knocking off a line or two to let you know how much I apprisiate it you sending me that wire on opening nite. Dont think because I didnt answer before I didnt apprisiate it because that is far from the case. But I guess you know that because if you knew when I was opening you surely must be aware how busy Ive been ever since opening nite. I figure you read in *Variety* what date I was opening in which case I figure you have seen the write ups since then telling how busy Ive been and believe me its no exagerton.

Well maybe it seems a long time since opening nite and in a way it does to me too. It will only be five weeks this coming Friday but it seems longer considering all that has happened to your old pal Joey. Its hard to believe that under two months ago Joey was strictly from hunger as they say but I was. The last time I saw you (August) remember the panic was on. I figured things would begin to break a little better around August but no. A couple spots where I figured I would fit in didnt open at all on acct of bankroll trouble and that was why I left town and came out this way. I figured you live in a small town in Michigan and you can stay away from the hot spots because there arent any and that way you save money. I was correct but I sure didnt figure the panic would stay on as long as it did. I finely sold the jalloppy and hocked my diamond ring the minute I heard there would be a chance down this way. I never was in Ohio before but maybe I will never be any place else. At least I like it enough to remain here the remainder of my life but of course if NBC is listening in Im only kidding.

Well I heard about this spot through a little mouse I got to know up in Michigan. She told me about this spot as it is her home town altho spending her vacation every year in Michigan. I was to a party one nite (private) and they finely got me to sing a few numbers for them and the mouse couldn't take her eyes off me. She sat over in one corner of the room not paying any attenton to the dope she was with until finely it got so even he noticed it and began making cracks but loud. I burned but went on singing and playing but he got too loud and I had to stop in the middle of a

number and I said right at him if he didnt like it why
didnt he try himself. Perhaps he could do better. The
others at the party got sore at him and told him to
pipe down but that only made him madder and the
others told me to go ahead and not pay any attenton
to him. So I did. Then when I got finished with a few
more numbers I looked around and the heel wasnt
there but the mouse was. She didnt give me a hand
but I could tell she was more impress than some that
were beating their paws off. So I went over to her and
told her I was sorry if it embarrassed her me calling
attention to her dope boy friend but she said he wasnt a
boy friend. I said well I figured that. I said she looked
as if she could do better than him and she said, "you
for instance" and I said well yes. We laughed and
got along fine and I took her home. She was staying
with her grandmother and grandfather, two respectible
old married people that lived there all their life. They
were too damn respectible for me. They watched her
like a hawk and one oclock was the latest she could
be out. That to me is the dumbest way to treat that
kind of a mouse. If its going to happen it can happen
before nine oclock and if it isnt going to happen it
isnt going to no matter if you stay out till nine oclock
the next morning. But whats the use of being old if you

cant be dumb? So anyway Nan told me about this spot
down here and knew the asst mgr of the hotel where
the spot is and she said she would give me a send in
and if I didnt hold them up for too much of the ready
she was sure I could get the job. I sing and play every
afternoon in the cocktail bar and at night I relieve the
band in the ballroom. Anyway I figured I would have
to freshen up the old wardrobe so I had to get rid of
the jalloppy and hock my diamond ring. I made the
trip to Ohio with Nan in her own jalloppy which isnt
exactly a jalloppy I might add. Its a 37 Plymouth
conv coop. It took us three days to go from Mich. to
Ohio but Ill thank you not to ask any questions about
my private life.

This asst mgr auditioned me when we finely arrived
and I knew right away I was in because he asked me
for a couple of old numbers like Everybody Step and
Swanee and a Jerry Kern medley and he was a Car-
michael fan. Everything he asked me for I gave him
and of course I put up a nice appearance being sun-
burned and a white coat from the proseeds of selling
the jalloppy and hocking the ring. I rehearsed with
the band altho Collins the leader hates my guts and
finely I talked this asst mgr into letting me do a single
irregardless of the band and he did.

Well you might say I ran the opening nite. I m.c'd and they had a couple kids from a local dancing school doing tap, one of them not bad altho no serious competiton for Ginger Rogers. They were only on for the first week. They also had another mouse who was with the band, living with the drummer. She tried to be like Maxine. Well she wasnt even colored, thats how much like Maxine she was. The local 400 turned out for the opening nite and inside a week I was besieged with offers to entertain at private parties which I do nearly every Sunday as the bar and ballroom are not open Sunday or at least I do not work. In additon to the job at the hotel and the private parties you probably have read about the radio job. I went on sustaining the first week and by the end of the second week I got myself a nice little commercial. I am on just before the local station hooks up with NBC Blue Network five nites a week but I dont think you can catch me in New York. Not yet! My sponsor is the Acme Credit Jewellery Company but I only have eight more weeks to go with them then I am free to negosiate with a better sponsor. Still Im not complaining. Your old pal Joey is doing all right for himself. I get a due bill at the hotel and what they pay me in additon aint hay. I also have the radio spot and the private parties. I went for a second hand Lasalle coop and I am thinking of joining the country club. I go there all the time with some of the local 400 so I figure I might as well join but will wait till I make sure I am going to stay here. I get my picture in the paper and write ups so much that I dont even bother to put them in my scrap book any more.

The crowd at the club are always ribbing me about it and accuse me of having the reporters on my payroll but I just tell them no, not the reporters, the editors. I am a little sore at one of the papers because the local Winchell links my name constantly with the name of a very sweet kid that I go to the club and play golf with. Not that it isnt true. We see each other all the time and she comes to the hotel practically every nite with a party and when Im through for the nite we usely take a ride out to a late spot out in the country. Her father is president of the second largest bank. It is the oldest. The biggest bank was formally two banks but they merged. Her name is Jean Spencer and a sweeter kid never lived. I really go for her. But this local Winchell took a personal dislike to me and made a couple cracks about us. One was "That personality boy at a downtown hotel has aired the femme that got him the job and is now trying to move into society."

Me trying to move in to society! Society moved in on me is more like it. Jean was burned because she was afraid her father might see the item and when I meet her father I dont want him to have the wrong impression. I think the colyumist got the item from my ex-friend Nan. I didnt see much of her when I was rehearsing and the afternoon of opening nite she called up and said she wanted to come but what the hell could I do? Ask for a big table when they were getting $5 a head cover charge? I was glad enough to get the job without asking too many favors. Then a week or so later she called up and asked me could I let her have $50. I asked her what for and she hung up. Well if she didnt even want to do me the curtesy to tell me what for I wasnt going to follow her around begging her to take it. But I gave it a few days thought and decided to let her have it but when I phoned her they said she quit her job and left town. I understand from Schall the asst mgr that she sold her Plymouth and went to N.Y. Her name is Nan Hennessey so if you run into her anywhere youll know her. She could be worse, that is worse on the eye, a little dumb tho.

Well pally, they will be billing me for stealing all their writing paper if I dont quit this. Just to show you I dont forget I inclose $30. Ill let you have the rest as soon as possible. Any time I can help you out the same way just let me know and you can count on me. I guess you kissed that fifty goodbye but that isnt the way I do things. But I guess you know that, hey pal?

All the best from

PAL JOEY

Ex-Pal

Dear Friend Ted:

That is if I can call you friend after the last two weeks for it is a hard thing to do considering. I do not know if you realize what has happen to me oweing to your lack of consideraton. Maybe it is not lack of consideraton. Maybe it is on purpose. Well if it is on purpose all I have to say is maybe you are the one that will be the loser and not me as I was going to do certan things for you but now it does not look like I will be able to do them.

Let us rehearse the whole thing briefley. I wrote to you on the 26 or 7 of last month telling you how I was getting along and inclosing $30 and telling you all the news out here about me getting this radio job and singing in the hotel. Also telling you I was going around with a girl in the local 400 who had a father a banker et cetra. Then I also made the unfortunate error of telling you to look up a certain mouse if you happen to come across her. Which did and mentoned my name. Well theres the rub. Oweing to your lack of consideraton (mentoning my name) there is hell to pay and I will tell you why. Maybe you know why. Maybe you knew damn well what you were doing and maybe not but any how I will tell you just in case.

The way I get it you meet this mouse and right off you shoot off your face about I wrote you and told you to look her up and she gets the wrong impresson because as I understand it she thinks you think all you have to do is menton my name and you are in. Then she gets sore as hell and decides to get even with me. Well here I am 1000 miles from N. Y. and doing OK with my radio job and singing at the hotel and with this kid that has a father a banker and out of the blue everything goes haywire. You knew damn well the mouse I told you about was from this town because I remember distintly telling you all about her in my letter of the 26 or 7. I remember distintly telling you she was no tramp and you only drew your own conclusons and not from anything I told you. So here I am doing OK with a car and two good jobs and this society kid going for me and what happens. This is what happens. I do not know what because it is too earley to say.

First of all the asst mgr of the hotel where I am

singing he comes to me and says "Joey I just rec'd informaton that is not doing you any good around this
town and I want you to level with me and tell me if
it is true." What? I said. What informaton? "Well I
do not exactly know how to put it man to man. We are
both men of the world but this is what I have reference to, meaning that a certan mouse from this town
had to leave town on acc't of you and is now in N. Y.
and instead of helping her you are writing letters to
pals in N. Y. and shooting off your face about what a
don Juan you are. That dont do you any good personally and I will state frankly that while we are
highly pleased with your singing and drawing power as
a personality here at the hotel however we have to look
at it from all the angels and once it gets around that
you are the kind of chap that writes letters to his pals
in N. Y. mentoning his fatal attracton to the ladies
why some nite some guy is just going to get his load
on and you are singing and a guy will walk up and
take a poke at you while you are singing. Think it
over" he said. Well this asst mgr is a pal of mine and I
have the deepest respect for him and I went on & did
a couple numbers and after I went to him and got him
to tell me all about it. In detail.

So you call yourself a pal. Well that mouse I told

you to look up knew this asst mgr in fact I think I told you she introduce me to him. I can see it all clearly. You met her and moved in and then you told her I told you all about her and the little trip we took on the way down from Michigan. As if that wasnt enough the next thing you do you have to destroy the only fine decent thing that has happen to me since coming to this jerk town, namely Jean. Jean is the girl that has a father a banker and it was only a queston of time before I was to meet the family and from there it was only a queston of time before things came to the definitely serious stage, but boy you certanly louse that up. I was to accompany Jean to a private party last Tues. nite and she would pick me up at the hotel after I did a couple numbers and go to this party. Usully when she picks me up she is with another couple but last Tues. when the doorman sent in word she was there she was alone in her Packard conv coop. I thought nothing of it till I notice she was not driving in the directon of this private party and also not opening her trap but just driving and I called her attenton to the fact. "No. We are not going to Dwight and Connie Reynolds party this evening" she said. I thought maybe it was called off and said so but she said no it was not called off but she wanted to talk with me. Then out it came. Thanks to you she gets this annonamous letter from that mouse I told you about saying to look out for me that I was a guy that would move in on her and then shoot off my face about it all over. I ask her if I could see the letter and she said she tore it up and I said did she look at the postmark. "Was it postmark N. Y.?" I said. She said no, here, but of course that mouse would send it to some girl friend here and get it postmark here. Well Jean & I had quite a scene much as I dislike scenes and no am't of persuason on my part would convince her it was the work of a lousy bitch that all she was was jealous. "To think that I was on the vurge of inviting you to Sunday dinner next Sunday" she said. That shows how things stood between she & I, but so that is all loused up too.

Well I was frantic. I had come to care deeply for Jean. She lives in a very different world than you and I. Her father is this banker and very conservative and not use to having his daughter going around with chaps that sing in a hotel even if it is one of the principle hotels in the mid west. I go out with all the best people here the 400 but not the older crowd & just on the vurge of going to Jeans house for Sunday dinner she gets this annonamous letter sticking the shiv in my back. Thanks to you. Well I thought for a minute

maybe the mouse came home & sent the letter herself
and I gave her a buzz Wed. afternoon and a dame's
voice answered and when she said who was it I told
her and it turned out to be the sister of the one that
is causeing all the trouble. When I told her who I was
she called me everything she could think of till I
thought if anybody was listening in they would think
they were over-hearing some bag and that she probably is because you got to be a bag to know some of the
things she called me. She also made threats and said
one of these nites she was coming down to the hotel
when I was doing a number and would personally spit
in my eye and knock me the hell off the stand. Then I
told her what I thought of her *and* her sister and if
she ever showed her face around the hotel I would
knock her teeth down her throat. Woman or no woman.
I shut her up the bitch. I said she and her fine feath-
ered sister. Well I said if she wanted to know anything about her sister ask anybody that was in Michigan last summer and she would find out what I meant.
So if you see the mouse again you can tell her. I dont
give a damn if I lose my job here at the hotel or the
radio spot. I dont have to take that stuff from any
mouse or her sister. As for you my ex-pal you know
what you can do and also you can sing for the $20 I

owe you. I am making a little trip to N. Y. in the near future and we will have a little talk and you can explain your positon, altho the way I feel now if I saw you now your positon would be horizontle. I might as well tell you I am going to the gym 3 or 4 times a week and not that I need it because I always could slap you around when ever I wanted to.

You know what you can do.

YOUR EX-PAL JOEY

How I Am Now in Chi

PAL TED:

Well, pally, I have come to the concluson that old pals are best and never put too much faith in new acquaintances or you will end up two away from the 9 ball. When I tell you that you are getting it straight from head-quarters, because I know. I have been thinking it over and the true test of friendship is if you can weather such things as for instance you and I, meaning like differences of opinon over a mouse or the dough department and things on that order. You and I certanly have had our differences of opinon over the above yet here I am when I think it over and give the matter mature consideraton I think of you as a friend and I always hope you will consider me a friend if you have the ill fortune of ever getting in a spot in which I found myself recently. Then you can count on me altho' hoping the occason does not arise. (God forbid.)

Well I recall telling you about a little mouse one of the local 400 that her father was president of the

bank (largest in town). This mouse Jean by name use
to come every night to the hotel to hear me sing and it
got so it was embarrasing owing to the fact that those
lugs in the band would begin to kid me about it. They
would say that mouse has got it for Joey but bad. She
would come there and sit and just look at me and when
she would get up to dance and I would sing and she
would just stand there in front of me with her escort
and it became so that it was obvious and altho' I pride
myself on being equal to such situatons (having had
the experience before) it use to disconcert me more
than I can say. However she arranged an introducton
and I use to take her out especially when I was singing
at private parties of the local 400. In a short time she
use to stop for me at the hotel damn near every evening and I came to care for her as she was different
than the usual ones that make a fool of themselves
over a singer or entertainer. We were reaching the
stage where it was you might say only a queston of
time before Joey and Jean would veil up and perhaps
I would consider giving up this life. Not that I ever
intended doing that but she use to discuss it with me.
She often use to ask me if I thought my life interesting and was it fun and how did I happen to get in it
and of course that was her subtile way of getting me to

consider probably going into the banking game with
her father after we got married.

Well of course she was nineteen years old and one
for the book as far as looks, figure, personality is concerned and also had plenty of scratch, being the bank
presidents daughter. I went to work and bought a
couple new arrangements in fact she gave me one for
Xmas last Xmas. I happen to say one night I needed a
couple new arrangements and she asked me how much
they were and I told her my guy charged $50. She
also gave me a set of studs and cuff links to wear with
my tails that must have set her back the price of four
arrangements. It was her favorite song at the time,
the arrangement she gave me. It was You go to my
Head. I had an old arrangement of it from last summer but never had any call for it but she use to like it
before she met me and so I got out the old arrangement and of course did not spoil it for her by saying it
was one I had last summer and never had any call for.
However I used the 50 to give her a Xmas present, a
sport watch.

Then around the end of January they were having
this ball in honor of the President (Roosevelt) to get
up a fund that they would give for this infantile parala-
sys. Very white of them as they sit around all year and

say what a heel he is and on his birthday they give him this ball and it is a club called the Junior League that she belonged .to had charge of getting the talent and all that like publicity etc. So of course I gladly donated my services as I was going anyway having planned to escort Jean to the ball. The ball was in the ballroom of the hotel but I was going to escort her from her house. Then at the very last minute I said to her what should we do that evening until it was time to go to the ball (11.30 or 12) and she said she was going to a dinner party at these friends of hers named Fenton. I said it was a fine time to tell me that and said I consider it a fine thing to go to the Fenton's for dinner knowing that they were one of the few that took a snobbish attitude in connecton with me. I told her she could take it or leave it and if she went to their house for dinner she could count me out on the subject of escorting her to the ball. I was plenty burned and she said she never understood I was taking her anyway and of course she was right. I took it for granted and didnt bother to ask her until the last minute and then I said well I will just stop for you at the Fenton's about 11.30 and that will save you the trouble of coming to the ball alone or with another couple. Imagine my surprise to learn that she already had an

escort, Jerry Towle a young dope that does nothing but
fly his own plane and scaring farmer's horses and always in some kind of a jam with the law but his old
man has plenty of scratch and gets him out of it. I said
you go with Towle and let him take you every other
place from now on and I said and dont bother to come
to the hotel any more but stay away and our date for
the next night was off.

Well we had a quarrel about that and it ended up
I didnt go to the Fenton's and when I was singing that
night at the ball she made Towle dance her up and
request Go to my Head but I said very politely I only
had the newer numbers and did not sing Go to my
Head this year. Did she burn? I didn't even dance
with her and I only sat with the boys in the band all
night and then went up to my room after I did my
numbers and called up some hustler and took her to
a hamburger joint where the 400 go every night after
dances and hoped Jean and Towle would come in but
they never did so I gave the hustler 5 bucks for her
time and sent her home in a taxi.

Well the next night I am singing and in she comes
but I never give her a tumble but she gets her load on
I notice and about one a.m. a note comes over by waiter
and she wants me to meet her but she is with this party

and I am burned so I dont answer the note. I just tell the waiter no reply and when I finish my last number I screw and go around the corner to have a cup of coffee and there she is, followed me. I do not want to make a scene then and there and she has her load on and will not go back and rejoin her party so I send around and get my car out of the garage hoping to take her for a ride and sober her up but oh no. Instead we go for a ride and altho' it was freezing and we did not have a coat either of us we are out for about an hour and always fighting and it began to get late and I knew the grill at the hotel would be putting the chairs up on the tables so I ignored her and turned around and went back. No sign of her party. They have gone. That means I have to take her home and she lives out in the suburbs and by the time we get there somebody has called her up to see if she got home and woke up the old man and he is waiting for her in a dressing gown. She is still plastered the little lush and her old man asks what the meaning of this is and who am I and bringing his daughter home in this conditon. Then I tell him who I am and he says Oh, he has heard about me and has always wanted to meet me and without any warning brings one up from the floor and I stop it with my chin, as dirty a punch as I ever saw. I got up but had the presence of mind so that I did not let him have one but said I dont want any part of his daughter, the lush. Keep her home or he would be a grandfather one of these days without a son in law. I think he would have got a gun but I was out of there before he had the chance.

Well the next a.m. about 10 the phone rings and it is the manager, my boss. He wants me down in his office so I go and he hears all about it only an exageraton of what really happened. To make a long story short I am out. I say what about my contract and he says read your contract and then I remember he had the right to fire me if I get out of line and he gives me the rest of the week (pay) and an extra week and says he advised me to lam out of there as I insulted the most powerful man in the whole town as I will soon find out. I find out alright. I call up this ad agency that pays me for singing on the local radio staton where my sponsor is this credit jewelry company. They were just about to call me. I am out. The mouse's old man only owns the God damn staton. I go to a lawyer but he wont take my case as he says I havent any case. Even if I had he would think twice about bucking this mouse's old man. So there I am holding an empty bag with my wardrobe and a car only about half paid for and all told about a little over 300 in my kick. So I go back to the hotel and start in packing (about 5 in the afternoon this is) and a messenger comes and brings me a note from Jean. She is sorry about it and did not want to cause me all this trouble and would do anything to make or mend. Her old man had her at the doctor's or she would have got in touch with me sooner and will I call her at this number, a girl friend of hers. They are going to take her to some place in N. Carolina the next day and she has to see me. I do not have to worry as the dr. says she is okay, but she would not be able to stand it going away like this with me feeling this way all over a little thing like a misunderstanding over the Fenton's dinner and she heard her old man threaten to get me bounced out of town etc and she is desperate because she loves me. Well I thought it over and what a fine chance I had to show her old man who was the most powerful man in town as far as his own family are concerned. All I had to do was pick up Jean and drive over the state line and inside of two hours he would have a son in law alright. I am sitting there debating within myself as to whether I will call her or not and the door opens. "You know me," he says. Towle. "I see you are packing. Good. There is a 9 oclock for Chicago and an 8.30 for N. Y.

and I would suggest the 8.30 but I leave the choice entirely up to you." he says. "I think I will sit around and take you to the train." I ignore him but go on packing and when I finish up I send down and have room service bring me up a steak sandwich with French fries, a cup of coffee and a piece of pie and I eat it there with him sitting there. I had to pay cash for it as room service will not let me sign. Then I lit a butt and smoke it calmly and then I phone the railroad and order a lower on the 9 oclock for Chi. I can see he is burned but that is what I intend. Then the phone rings and he answers it and says he is not here but has just left and then he says "Dont be a damn fool Jean this is Jerry and yes he is here but you are not going to see him if I can help it and you may not speak to him as I am acting on your fathers orders." Then he hangs up. He is a big lug. Over 200.

Well I phone the garage and tell them to put my car into dead storage and take out the battry and then it is time to go to the train and he goes with me. When we get there I tell him he can have the pleasure of paying the taxi and he says it is a pleasure alright and I said I thought it would be and also a pleasure for me. When I go to get my ticket he even pays for the ticket, tips the porter, etc. I did not lose my sense of humor. I said "By the way I have nothing to read on the train" and he buys me papers and magazines. I see the humor in it and I also say I always have chewing-gum on trains so he buys me some gum. But he does not see the humor for when the train is ready to pull out I reach out my hand and say it was a pleasure to have him come down and see me off, him of all people and just then he hauls off and slaps my hand, burned like I never saw anybody burned.

Well the train pulled out and that is the story of how I am now in Chi. I am singing for coffee & cakes at a crib on Cottage Grove Ave. here. It isnt much of a spot but they say it is lucky as four or five singers and musicians who worked here went from here to big things and I am hoping. Well give my best to Artie and Fred and Chink and Mort. Tell Mort congratulatons as I hear he is starting up a new band and I would be willing to work for scale. Tell Fred when he comes out to look me up as I plug his last two numbers every nite. Well Ted all the best and I don't have to say I think your solo in Jeepers Creepers is as good as Vanuti. I am glad a pal is having such good luck and I mean that sincerely as ever. Will write soon again.

PAL JOEY

Bow Wow

Dear Friend Ted:

Well pal I had to sit down the minute I came home just returning from a furniture store around the corner from where I am living. Having just heard what you did to Hong Kong Blues. Well if I was ever proud of a friend I am proud of you alright. To say it is a wonderful recording is to say the least. I happen to drop in at this store as I do every week to hear the new recordings. You know me, Ted. Strictly larceny when it comes to listening to those arrangements but I cant afford to buy any new arrangements of my own right now so I have to get them from recordings and take the best of this one and that one. The joint where I am singing and m. c-ing in is satisfied with my work and it keeps me in coffee & cakes but not much more. As a pal of mine said the other night Chicago is alright if you like Chicago altho I would rather be back in N. Y. or even go to Frisco for the other Fair. I have had one or two propositions in regards to Frisco but nothing attractive. That is to make it worth while going all the way out there and then maybe getting stuck where I dont know anybody. I dont know what to do so for the moment am sticking here getting my coffee & cakes and building up a local following. They have a place out on the North side that has made me one or two offers but I will stay down in this territory until I get a propositon from some place in the Loop dist. I figure I ought to go good in a place like the Chez Paris, tops here, or maybe one of the hotels. Downey always goes good here altho his stuff is of course different than mine. Well enough of my problems. I only wanted to conveigh my congratulations on the new recordings and for a young band. Who have you got on the guitar? If I didn't know McDonough was dead I would say it was him. I also thought I recognized Fud but I guess he is still with Tommy so guess I am an error.

Well I guess you wonder what I do with my spare moments out in this bailwick. Write letters is one thing. Just think a year ago you were the one crying the blues and less than a year ago I was doing alright with the Packard etc. And now you are up there and there will be no stopping you and believe me you have the ardent wishes of success from all your pals. I am getting by in this crib in Chi. but guess I have learned my lesson and am a changed man. All because of a dog.

Well this is the first time I wrote since I bo't Skippy the name of my dog and it is wonderful what they can do. They give you the courge to continue when things look bad. I use to hear Al White on the subject of man's best friend the dog and use to laugh myself sick when White would rib the love and affecton of a man and a dog but he is wrong. There is something to it. It worked in my case as when I came out here I didnt have any job and took the first thing that came along and took the attitude that the world was a pretty sorry place to live in and it effected my work. I would get up to do a number and I took the attitude that I hated all the people there and I guess it showed because Lang (no relaton to Eddie) the owner of this spot gave me a call. He said get more of a pleasing personality in it or pack. It put the fear of God in me as I wasnt there long enough to building up a following and had not stashed any dough away. Also no prospects or proposi-tons from other spots and of course this joint dont spend any dough advertising and the press agent gets no pay but only a certan am't of drinks on the cuff so you can imagine how hard he works. So I gave the matter my mature consideraton and then that week I was out getting my breakfast around 4 one afternoon and right near where I eat is this pet & dog shop. I never had any interest in dogs and never considered owning one and thought they were a nusaince especially in towns. But I saw this mouse standing there bent over and talking to one of the dogs in the window of the shop. She was about twenty and I didnt care if she had a face out of the Zoo but spring was in the air and this mouse had a shape that you dont see only on the second Tuesday of every week and when you do see a shape like that you have to do something about it. So I stopped and feined an interest in the dog kingdom and cased the mouse and got a look at her kisser. Well it fitted in with the rest of the body. Not pretty but cute. She had personality in her face I could see that. She didn't see me because she was so crazy about this one dog that had his nose up against the window and she was talking to it before she noticed me and then got sort of embarassed when she saw me. But by that time I was looking at the dog and smiling at him and leaned over and started talking and the first name I could think of came to my head and I said hello Skippy boy. And the mouse looked at me and said is that his name, Skippy? I said I didnt know I only pretend it was. I said I pass by here every day and got to love

him so much that I had to give him a name like the
name of an airdale dog I use to have when I was a
kid. Oh so I love dogs, she wanted to know and I said
yes. Then she said why didnt I buy this puppy and I
said for the same reason why I didnt buy a Dusenburg,
money. Well the effect it had on her was wonderful. I
could see tears in her eyes and she said it was a shame
that anybody that love dogs so much had to be de-
prived of them because of the finances where so many
people that didnt really love them had them and didnt
treat them properly. Yes, I said, that is true. I said I
was saving up so I could buy Skippy and there was a
sign in the window that said $30. That part was the
truth, that is, I didnt have any $30 to buy any dogs
with. I began telling her about Skippy the airdale that
I didnt have when I was a kid and pretty soon got to
believing it myself, all about how my heart was broken
when poor little Skippy was crushed beneath the wheels
of a 10 ton truck. I said my family were well to do
people in those days and wished to buy me another dog
but I said to them no dog would take the place of
Skippy and never would until one day I happen to be
going by this shop and my eye caught this little puppy's
and something about him reminded me of Skippy and
she said yes, he was a little like an airdale. Well I didnt

know an airdale from a hole in the ground and didnt
know what the hell this mut was in the window and so
I said it wasnt the breed, I said, it was just something
in this puppy's expresson that reminded me of my old
Skippy. She was touched. She said she never would of
taken me for somebody that loved dogs so much and I
said you don't know much about dogs then, Miss. I said
dogs have strange tastes in people and only a dog knows
who he likes. By this time Skippy was laying down and
I said he is tired and I said I had to go and get my
breakfast. I said this is the only time of the day that I
can see Skippy as they take them out of the window
soon. Just a guess but I didnt seem to remember seeing
the dogs in the window late in the afternoon and the
mouse said "Did I hear correctly when you said you
were going to have breakfast?" And I said yes, I am
one of those unusual people that their days are upside
down. I said you are probably the kind that would be
having tea now but I am having breakfast. That made
her laugh and so I took advantadge of that and said.
why not have tea with me if she didnt mind sitting at a
counter for it? As I said before I had cased this mouse
and she was pretty but I knew she was no society debu-
tante. Probably a stenog out of work but very cute. So
she said she often ate at counters and went with me.

I was right and she was a stenog looking for work. She went with me to this one-arm where I eat and she had a tomato on rye and a coffee and I had eggs and coffee and we started talking and it turned out she was from some little town in Illinois, not Peoria but some place like it. Her name was Betty Hardiman and lived with her married sister and her husband and only came to Chi a month before. I told her my people lost all their money in the crash and I had to leave Princeton college and go to work but the only work I was suited for was singing with a band or in a night club and then she said she recognized my name from passing the club on her way to the L. She said she thought people that worked in clubs got plenty of money and I said it depends on what club and then when it came time to pay the check she said she would pay her own and insisted and said let me consider that her contributon to buying Skippy.

Well I said I hoped she would come around to the club some time with her boy friend and I would sing any number she would request and she said her boy friend didnt live in Chi but went to college at the Illinois U. at Champaigne. I said well she should come some time with her sister and her husband and Betty said her bro. in-law never went to night clubs and I

said I guess it was pretty dreary for a young girl living
like that and she said it was becoming that way altho it
was better than home. She said she loved Chi, just
going around the Loop and watching the people's faces
on the L trains, but would like to see some more of the
fun but her boy friend was working his way thru the
Illinois U. and didnt get to Chi only two or three times
a year. Well I said this is very pleasant but I had to
go and rehearse a couple numbers at the club and got
her phone number and said I would like to take her
out some night if I got a night off and she said she tho't
it would be alright.

Well I saw her a couple times but only in the day
time. We use to meet at the dog shop. We would go
to the one-arm and then I would have to leave her but
one afternoon she borrowed her bro. in-law's car and
drove out to the country and I gave her a little going
over but not too much as I could tell the time was not
ripe. I was even surprised I could neck her at all on
acc't of this boy friend at the Illinois U, but I guess it
was the first time a pass was made at her since the last
time she saw the college boy and I guess she needed a
little workout. Well that night I hit a crap game for
about eighty clams and two days later I met Betty and
told her and she said now I could buy Skippy and I

said no, unfortunately the flea-bag where I was living
did not permit dogs. I said that was just my luck. Then
I said I have an idea. I said how about if I buy him
for her and she could keep him and on conditon that
she would let me see him and she said she would love
to but would have to ask her sister as they only had
an apartment. I met the sister by that time and I knew
she went for me but had not met the bro. in-law. She
asked the sister but the sister said no, Betty couldn't
have a dog in the ap't because it was too small, much as
she would love to have a dog. So then I went to my
landlady and asked her if I could have a dog and she
said sure so then I went to Betty and told her I had a
deal with my landlady that if I paid more rent I could
keep the dog so Betty was overjoyed and I bo't Skippy.
The landlady has a kid about ten or eleven and he takes
care of Skippy for me. Takes him for his walks and
washes him and the landlady thinks I am a fine young
fellow but why shouldnt she when her kid has the use
of a $30 dog for nothing. I often have fun with the
mut too and pat him and I often think if it wasn't for
Skippy I never would of met Betty. Her sister and
bro. in-law are going away the week-end after next and
we will have the ap't all to ourselves. It's about time
but I had to be patient as she said she wanted to be

sure first, but a man with such a love and affecton for dogs was a man you could trust. Well, pal, all the best and keep your eyes open for any spots you hear for me. I would rather be around N. Y. this summer as it gets hot as hell out here in summer but if you hear anything like a good spot with a band touring or some summer hotel in Mass. or Maine dont forget your pal. I have no contract here as they never heard of a contract at a crib like this so can leave at a moment's notice. Of course it will be worth sticking around a month or so if you get what I mean. Bow wow.

PAL JOEY

Give and Take

THE DOOR was opened and in came a woman in her late forties. She was carrying a cheap brief-case from which the varnish was peeling. She leaned forward with the weight of her front, although she was not exceptionally heavy behind. She wore silver-rimmed spectacles which made her eyes seem weak, until you really saw them, and then they were strong, bright, brown. She closed the door quietly, making a full half-turn in closing it. She was frowning a little, the way people sometimes do when they are trying not to make any noise. She went through the little foyer and came into the living-room and said "Oh!" in a shrill voice, and put her hand approximately over her heart and laughed. "Tommy. What are you doing up so early?"

"Hello, Mom," he said, very friendly. "I'm doing a little work on the claws." He looked at her—their eyes met—and then he went on filing his fingernails. He was wearing a blue pin-stripe suit, rather tight for his fat body. His legs were crossed. He was somewhere between twenty-five and thirty years old, and he had white, shiny skin, and as he filed his nails, four white, strong teeth clamped over his lower lip. "What's with you, Mom? How was school?"

"It's always the same. After the first year. And you know how long I've been at it." She took off her hat and put it on one of those little pedestals in the closet in the foyer. It was a hat that could just as well have been thrown on the floor. "What got you up so early? It's only a little after four."

"I couldn't sleep," said Tommy. "I just couldn't pound out any more after—oh, ten this morning. I didn't get up then. I stayed in the hay till around twelve-thirty, but then I thought, 'I'll get up.' So I did."

"Did you have any breakfast?"

"No scoff. Just a little mocha-java-coffee."

"And you've been in all this time?" said Mom.

"Well, no. I went out and shot a little game of pool and bought the aptanoon papers. Came home. Read the papers. Made a few phone calls. Then I remembered shooting pool how the claws looked. I don't know, Mom. I always look at other guys' fingernails to see if they got—you know—Burns Brothers. But my own, I don't hardly ever look at them."

"Don't hardly."

"Seldom."

Mom sat down comfortably and without grace, and began taking school papers out of the brief-case. "You're not broke, by any chance? That isn't why you stayed here till I came home?"

"Mom, I am. Last night I went out with Joey Forbstein, and there's a great student of the dollar. We went to a couple places, and every time a check came around, Joey recognized somebody that he thought he could put the touch on. So he'd get up and leave me with the bruise. Maybe he put the touch on these guys, but if he did, I never saw any of the gelt. He'd come back and I didn't want to ask him how he did, becuss that would look like I wanted him to pay the check. So."

"Why do you go out with people like that? For somebody that knows a lot about human nature!"

"That's it! Now Joey, for instance. Last night cost me—I mean extra, on account of Joey—about fifteen clams. Well, Joey's promoting a benefit for some cops up in Westchester some place. I go out with him. He rounds up maybe a half a dozen names. They promise to show at this benefit. What happens? Maybe four of them show. They get gold badges from the cops. Joey gets whatever he gets, but knowing Joey, I'd say the cops better bring their pistols when Joey gets to adding up the take. So Joey always does all right on the financial end. Comes away with five hundred dollars, say. I watch when this benefit is put on, and I know exactly when to go to Joey and say, 'Joey, I need a hunnerd and twenty-fi dollars.' Joey always overestimates what he's going to rob these cops of, so he gives me one two five. I do know human nature, Mom, because for instance if I ask Joe for one hundred, he'll say fifty. But one two five sounds like I needed one two five, and he lets me have it."

"And how do you pay him back? You don't."

"In favors, Mom. It's give and take. Don't you see that? I wouldn't think of taking that kind of money from Joey if I didn't know I could pay him back. Not in cash, necessarily. But I know people that sooner or later Joey has to get to. He *hass* to. Where could Joey get a pair of fight tickets at the last minute for nothing? Nowhere in the City of New York. But I just happen to know the right people. What if Joey has some enterprise that he has to see like somebody in the cops? I mean something legitimate, of course, but a lot of times time counts. For a nickel or a dime, the price of two phone calls, I save him endless bother. So in about two weeks I'm good for a hunnerd and twenty-fi dollars from Joey alone. When the time comes, he'll be around to ask his favor, and that means we're square. That is to *say*, Mom, on an investment of fifteen dollars, I get back one two five. Then I can pay you back if you need it."

"I only hope I don't need it. I can give you twenty-five dollars now."

"Make it twenty, Mom. Twenty is enough. Tonight I'll only need hat-check money, a taxi maybe. Tomorrow I have a dinner at the Astor to go to. Little Artie McFadden is putting on a dinner, and I got him a couple full-page ads for his program. My end ought to be twenty-fi dollars, and I know Artie's good for it."

"I'll have to give you a check," said Mom.

"A check's fine, Mom. And a quarter to get uptown. I kept looking at my fingernails shooting pool, and I didn't win a game."

Mom folded the papers and got up and went to the desk and wrote out a check. Tommy stood beside her with one hand on her shoulder. "Where the dough department is concerned, you're O.K., Mom," he said. "You're a fast man with a buck." She finished writing the check and handed it to him with her left hand. She kept looking at the inkwell.

"Tommy," she said, still looking at the inkwell.

"What, Mom?"

"Nothing," she said.

He stood there reading the check, holding it in both hands. "Oh, I know," he said. "But one of these days I'll hit." Then he went out, and the bow on his hatband was on the wrong side of his head.

The Gentleman in the Tan Suit

ROBERT, she supposed, was well dressed. Well dressed for San Francisco. He was not well dressed according to the standards Mary had had to adopt as Mr. Monkton's secretary. In the years that she had been Mr. Monkton's secretary Mary had had to learn about Charvet and Peal and those people. She knew how much it cost to have a pair of shoes sent back to Peal for rebuilding. She knew it cost two or three dollars more than the shoes Robert was wearing would cost new. Mr. Monkton was one of the best-dressed men downtown, and one thing she had noticed about Mr. Monkton's clothes was that no matter what he wore in the country (and she knew little enough about that), his city clothes were not the kind that would have to be pressed after a single wearing. That was the way Robert's clothes impressed her in the first few seconds. The suit was too light a tan, so light that she did not see how he could keep it clean after one ride in a taxi, and already it had wrinkles at the side of the knee and in the elbows that would not disappear into the cloth. She noticed that his shirt was only half a shade away from the tan of the suit; the tie was tan with white figures, the socks were silk, tan silk. The shoes were tan. The hat was tan, with only the beginning of finger marks where it was dented in the crown. Kay probably thought he dressed wonderfully. Mary thought it was awful.

Mary had come home and found him here. Not to her surprise; she knew they were coming, Kay and Robert. She had wondered a little about the young man's curiosity, what kind of curiosity would make him want to meet his wife's sister after he had been married a year, and make him want it so much that he would be willing to spend so much money. Mary had written in answer to Kay's letter, telling her that unless it was New York they wanted to see, why not save the money and she would come out to San Francisco when Mr. Monkton went abroad in October. But Kay had replied that all their plans had been made—Robert had made them. His pay cut had been restored, his father had given them money for a new car, which they did not need, and—this was something Mary supplied without any information from her younger sister —apparently they had not done any planning towards having a baby. The money was there, so Mary told them to come on.

Robert was alone in the apartment when Mary arrived there. He was sitting on the davenport, with one arm along the arm of the davenport, and the other arm along the back. It looked like a position that had just been assumed, but when Mary saw how many cigarettes had been smoked and noticed that there was no impression in any of the chairs or elsewhere in the davenport, she thought she had an idea what kind of young man her sister had married. She had seen many, many young men waiting for Mr. Monkton, sitting in that same position, not insulted when Mr. Monkton would go out with his hat on, ignoring them. They would wait in the reception-room for Mary and ask for another appointment, and another, if necessary, until Mr. Monkton would keep an appointment, or talk to them in the elevator or somewhere. Young men who sat that way almost always got to see Mr. Monkton. Usually that was as much as they did get, but Mary knew that they felt they had made a contact. And so Mary knew her sister had married a young man who knew how to wait. What they said about the men who made them wait was another matter; she had heard them more than once at Schrafft's and places like that, sometimes identifying Mr. Monkton by name: "Why, I waited for that bastard Monkton. . . ." Mary, when she wasn't too tired, delighted in passing close to young men whom she thus overheard, knowing they would recognize her and get the lump because they could not be sure she had not overheard them.

Robert turned his head when she let herself in the apartment. He did not stand until he had a look at her. He laughed and showed his teeth. Mary knew him for the kind of young man who would go to his dentist regularly just to be able to say (truthfully) that dentists would starve if everybody had teeth like his. His teeth were so good and so obviously good all the way back that there was no suspense to watching them. She wondered if he ever bit Kay.

"You're Mary, I'll bet," he said.

"Yes," she said. "And Robert. How are you, Robert? I'm so glad to see you." She struck the same note on glad and see, which took the curse off the sentence.

"I'm glad to see you, too, Mary," he said.

She wondered whether there was any special reason, the way he said it. They shook hands a long time, and his not kissing her right away was something in his favor. "Do I kiss my sister-in-law?" he said.

"Mm-hmm." She extended her cheek.

He was a little embarrassed after kissing her. "That's the first girl outside of Kay I've kissed since God knows when. Anyway two years is a conservative estimate."

What did he want? Did he want her to relay that to Kay, or was he lying, or was he trying to boast about his fidelity? "Well, that's pretty good for these times," she said.

"Good, hell, it's perfect," he said. "Kay will be here any minute. She's supposed to be here now, but I guess she had to stop and buy something, is my guess."

"How about a cocktail?"

"Not for me, thanks," he said. "If you want one."

"We'll wait till Kay gets here, then," she said.

"I only drink beer except on state occasions. Not that this—"

"Well, I should think!"

"Well, you know, like football games or sumpn. Kay likes a cocktail, though. You bet. She makes about the only decent cocktail I ever drank. She's going to be awfully glad to see you. Gee, five years. I guess she was only eighteen when you saw her last time."

"You understand about my not going home for the wedding, don't you, Robert?"

"Sure. I said to Kay, I said, 'Listen, a job's a job

these days. You can't expect your sister to just up and—' "

"Oh. Did you have to explain? I mean apologize for me?"

"Well, frankly, you know. It's a year ago now, so it's all over and done with, but, yes, in a way. I didn't have to—you wouldn't call it apologize, but Kay couldn't get it through her head that you couldn't just up and go, right in the middle of winter. I said to her, 'Listen,' I said, 'this Mr. Monkton'—your boss—'I happen to know he's a big shot, and secretary to him probably means a twenty-four-hour-a-day job.' She got it finally. Hell, your aunt and uncle, they were swell." He stopped abruptly and sat down. He looked up at Mary. "You know what?"

"What?"

"You know what suddenly occurred to me—oh, after we were married. I don't know how to put this."

"You can say anything to me."

"Well, I didn't realize till after we were married why she wanted you to be there." He shook his head. "You know, Kay didn't know a god-damn thing. You know?"

"Oh." She sat beside him. "I thought girls today—

I suppose I've been living in New York such a long time."

"Not Kay. And your aunt never told her anything."

"But twenty-two years old."

"That's what I thought."

"Oh, I should have gone home. How about now?"

He smiled. "Okay now. Yes, she's all right now. We've been married a year, you know." He stood up. "Well, I guess this is a hell of a way to talk the first ten minutes I meet my wife's sister. But that was the only thing—I admit I sort of held it against you myself, but I don't any more."

"I *couldn't* be so thoughtless."

"*It's* all right," he said. "Honestly, there's nothing to worry about any more. See, it's all *right* now, so I thought Kay and I—it'd be a good idea for her to come East and see you, now that everything's all right."

Mary looked at him and burst into tears.

Good-by, Herman

ILLER was putting his key in the lock. He had two afternoon papers folded under one arm, and a package—two dress shirts which he had picked up at the laundry because he was going out that night. Just when the ridges of the key were fitting properly, the door was swung open and it was his wife. She was frowning. "Hello," he said.

She held up her finger. "Come in the bedroom," she said. She was distressed about something. Throwing his hat on a chair in the foyer, he followed her to the bedroom. She turned and faced him as he put down his bundle and began taking off his coat.

"What's up?" he said.

"There's a man in there. He came to see you. He's been here for an hour and he's driving me crazy."

"Who is he? What's it all about?"

"He's from Lancaster, and he said he was a friend of your father's."

"Well, has he been causing any trouble?"

"His name is Wasserfogel, or something like that."

"Oh, hell. I know. Herman Wasservogel. He was my father's barber. I knew he was coming. I just forgot to tell you."

"Oh, you did. Well, thanks for a lovely hour. Hereafter, when you're expecting somebody, I wish you'd let me know beforehand. I tried to reach you at the office. Where were you? I tried everywhere I could think of. You don't know what it is to suddenly have a perfectly strange man—"

"I'm sorry, darling. I just forgot. I'll go in."

He went to the living-room, and there sat a little old man. In his lap was a small package, round which he had wrapped his hands. He was looking down at the package, and there was a faint smile on his face, which Miller knew to be the man's customary expression. His feet, in high, black shoes, were flat on the floor and parallel with each other, and Miller guessed that this was the way the little old man had been sitting ever since he first arrived.

"Herman, how are you? I'm sorry I'm late."

"Oh, that's all right. How are you, Paul?"

"Fine. You're looking fine, Herman. I got your letter and I forgot to tell Elsie. I guess you know each other by now," he said as Elsie came into the room and sat down. "My wife, Elsie, this is Herman Wasser-vogel, an old friend of mine."

"Pleased to meet you," said Herman.

Elsie lit a cigarette.

"How about a drink, Herman? A little schnapps? Glass of beer?"

"No, thank you, Paul. I just came; I wanted to bring this here. I just thought maybe you would want it."

"I was sorry I didn't see you when I was home for the funeral, but you know how it is. It's such a big family, I never got around to the shop."

"Henry was in. I shaved him three times."

"Yes, Henry was there longer than I was. I was only there overnight. I had to come right back to New York after the funeral. Sure you won't have a beer?"

"No, I just wanted to bring this in to give to you." Herman stood up and handed the little package to Paul.

"Gee, thanks a lot, Herman."

"What's that? Mr. Wasserfogel wouldn't show it to me. It's all very mysterious." Elsie spoke without look-ing at Herman, not even when she mentioned his name.

"Oh, he probably thought I'd told you."

Herman stood while Paul undid the package, revealing a shaving mug. "This was my father's. Herman shaved him every day of his life, I guess."

"Well, not every day. The Daddy didn't start shaving till he was I guess eighteen years old, and he used to go away a lot. But I guess I shaved him more than all the other barbers put together."

"Damn right you did. Dad always swore by you, Herman."

"Yes, I guess that's right," said Herman.

"See, Elsie?" said Paul, holding up the mug. He read the gold lettering: " 'J. D. Miller, M.D.' "

"Mm. Why do you get it? You're not the oldest boy. Henry's older than you," said Elsie.

Herman looked at her and then at Paul. He frowned a little. "Paul, will you give me a favor? I don't want Henry to know it that I give you this mug. After the Daddy died, I said, 'Which one will I give the mug to?' Henry was entitled to it, being the oldest and all. In a way he should have got it. But not saying anything against Henry—well, I don't know."

"Mr. Wasserfogel liked you better than he did Henry, isn't that it, Mr. Wasserfogel?" said Elsie.

"Oh, well," said Herman.

"Don't you worry, Herman, I'll keep quiet about it. I never see Henry anyway," said Paul.

"The brush I didn't bring. Doc needed a new one this long time, and I used to say to him, 'Doc, are you so poor yet you won't even buy a new shaving brush?' 'I am,' he'd say to me. 'Well,' I said, 'I'll give you one out of my own pocket for a gift.' 'You do,' he'd say, 'and I'll stop coming here. I'll go to the hotel.' Only joking, we were, Mrs. Miller. The Doc was always saying he'd stop coming and go to the hotel, but I knew better. He was always making out like my razors needed sharpening, or I ought to get new lights for my shop, or I was shaving him too close. Complain, complain, complain. Then around the first of last year I noticed how he'd come in, and all he'd say was, 'Hello, Herman. Once over, not too close,' and that's all he'd say. I knew he was a sick man. He knew it, too."

"Yes, you're right," said Paul. "When'd you get in, Herman?"

"Just today. I came by bus."

"When are you going back? I'd like to see some more of you before you go away. Elsie and I, we're going out tonight, but tomorrow night—"

"Not tomorrow night. Tomorrow night is Hazel's," said Elsie.

"Oh, I don't have to go to that," said Paul. "Where are you stopping, Herman?"

"Well, to tell you the truth, I ain't stopping. I'm going back to Lancaster this evening."

"Why, no! You can't. You just got here. You ought to stick around, see the sights. Come down to my office and I'll show you Wall Street."

"I guess I know enough about Wall Street; all I want to know. If it wasn't for Wall Street, I wouldn't be barbering at my age. No. Thanks very much, Paul, but I got to get back. Got to open the shop in the morning. I only have this relief man for one day. Young Joe Meyers. He's a barber now."

"Well, what the hell? Keep him on for another day or two. I'll pay him. You've got to stick around. How long is it since you've been to New York?"

"Nineteen years last March I was here, when young Hermie went to France with the Army."

"Herman had a son. He was killed in the war."

"He'd be forty years old, a grown man," said Herman. "No. Thank you, Paul, but I think I better be going. I wanted to take a walk down to where the bus leaves from. I didn't get my walk in today yet, and that will give me the chance to see New York City."

"Oh, come on, Herman."

"Don't be so insistent, Paul. You can see Mr. Was-serfogel wants to go back to Lancaster. I'll leave you alone for a few minutes. I've got to start dressing. But not too long, Paul. We've got to go all the way down to Ninth Street. Good-by, Mr. Wasserfogel. I hope we'll see you again sometime. And thank you for bring-ing Paul the cup. It was very sweet of you."

"Oh, that's all right, Mrs. Miller."

"Well, I really must go," said Elsie.

"I'll be in in a minute," said Paul. "Herman, you sure you won't change your mind?"

"No, Paul. Thank you, but I have the shop to think of. And you better go in and wash up, or you'll catch the dickens."

Paul tried a laugh. "Oh, Elsie isn't always like that. She's just fidgety today. You know how women get."

"Oh, sure, Paul. She's a nice girl. Very pretty-look-ing. Well."

"If you change your mind—"

"Nope."

"We're in the phone book."

"Nope."

"Well, just remember, if you *do* change your mind;

and I really don't know how to thank you, Herman. You know I mean it, how much I appreciate this."

"Well, your Dad was always good to me. So were you, Paul. Only don't tell Henry."

"That's a promise, Herman. Good-by, Herman. Good luck, and I hope I'll see you soon. I may get down to Lancaster this fall, and I'll surely look you up this time."

"Mm. Well, *auf Wiedersehen*, Paul."

"*Auf Wiedersehen*, Herman."

Paul watched Herman going the short distance to the elevator. He pushed the button, waited a few seconds until the elevator got there, and then he got in without looking back. "Good-by, Herman," Paul called, but he was sure Herman did not hear him.

I Could Have Had a Yacht

W HAT do you do?" I said to him. "Do you just sit around and drink coffee all night long till daylight?" He looked at me kind of funny, the most amazing look, and I thought he didn't understand me. "Is that all you do?" I said, and repeated my question, "Don't you ever do anything but sit around and drink coffee all night?" I said. I said, "I should think the waiters'd get sick and tired of looking at you, drinking coffee. What *is* it?" I said.

"Darling," he said, looking at me just as dead pan as I don't know what. "Darling, you mustn't worry so about me," he said. Well, I told him, I said I wasn't worrying about him. God forbid. Me worry about just some ordinary piano-player? I guess he is like Terry said. He has to put everything on a personal basis, right away. There I'd only been with him, I mean been in his *company*, just that one night, and I asked him a casual question and he wants to build up a great big love affair out of it or something. At least that's the impression I gathered by his remark, otherwise

why would he say like that, "Darling, don't worry so
about me"? I wasn't worrying about him, I was only
trying to make casual repartee so's the both of us
wouldn't sit there like two mummies. I wasn't worrying about him. I wasn't even thinking about him when
I said it if he wanted to know the truth, but naturally
when you're with a man like that, sitting in Dave's or
any place, and he doesn't carry on a conversation, naturally you try to make conversation by finding out if
you have interests in common that the two of you can
talk about, because otherwise you just *sit* there and it
looks terrible to see two people sitting in a restunt the
man drinking one cup of coffee after the other and
smoking these cigars and not saying anything. Right
away he wants to put everything on a personal basis
and I practically had to tell him I just wasn't innarested.

Like he said to me on the way home in the taxi. He
was sitting there with the cigar in his mouth and not
even condescending to hold up his end of the conversation except yes or no once in a while, and then this all
of a sudden he said, "Say, Toots, you have a nice pair
of gams." "Oh," I said. "I have a nice pair of gams."
I said to him, "Aren't you old eagle eye, though? You
been to the show three nights in succession, if one is

to believe your story," I said, "and," I said, "just now you notice I have nice legs. Where were you looking if you're just finding that out?" I said. I said, "Mr. Carroll thinks so, too, and so do a lot of other people that I'd take their word for it sooner than I would yours. Where were you looking all the time?" "Not at your legs," he said.

You know I asked a lot of other musicians about him. I asked them if they knew this fellow, and they all did. As a rule I wouldn't even spit on a musician. You know what they did to a friend of mine, don't you? Priscilla Wortman. She was with a unit that played, you know, the movie houses around. Boston, Chicago, Baltimore. You know. One of those units. So Priscilla, every town she went to—first of all I ought to tell you. The show opened in Pittsburgh, the unit did, and played there a week, and Priscilla had a great big mad love affair with a trumpet-player there. But gave! Then the unit played I think Boston, and so on. Well, every town they went to, always one of the musicians would make a big play for Priscilla, and after they were on the road a month or so, Priscilla began to notice that it was always a trumpet-player that made a play for her. Always a trumpet-player. Well, so when they played Chicago they were held

over a couple weeks in the same theatre, and Priscilla
went out with this trumpet-player in the theatre, and
she kind of fell for him, about this much. And one
night he got a little drunkie and he told her plenty.
He got sore at her for something and he told her
plenty, right before a room full of people. Explained
why trumpet-players always took her out. You know
what? This guy in Pittsburgh, or wherever it was, he
wrote on the music: "For a good time get the brunette
third from the right in the military number." And of
course every town the unit went to the trumpet-player
in that town would see this note on the music, and he'd
make a play for Priscilla. And by the time the unit
reached Chicago the trumpet-players in all the towns
had put okay and the name of the town on the music,
to show that they all agreed with the original one. So
when they went to Detroit and the trumpet-player
there asked her to go out with him you bet Priscilla
told him what she thought of him and all trumpet-
players in general. If it'd of been me I'd have made
them get new music, but Priscilla isn't equipped with
much up here.

So ever since I heard that story I wouldn't even spit
on a musician, but I had to find out about this Jack. I
wanted to know if they ever heard of him, *and,* they

all did. Some of them even stuck up for him. He wrote "Blue Moon." . . . No? Well, it had Blue in the title. I guess it wasn't "Blue Moon." Blue something. Who wrote the "Rhapsody in Blue"? I know it wasn't this Jack, but the one he wrote is *like* the "Rhapsody in Blue," so he must be very well known in those circles. Not that that impresses me. You have to be more than a musician to impress me. I could have had a yacht, so it takes more than a musician to impress me, but I must admit I like his attitude. He said to me the other night—oh, I see him. I see him two or three times a week. I didn't see him Tuesday of this week, so it isn't every night. But I was gunna say, the other night he said to me, "Darling," he said, "don't talk. Just don't talk," he said, "just be beautiful." And that's a nice compliment, you know. We have things in common, I can see that, but if he only wouldn't make these crypty remarks all the time.

Richard Wagner: Public Domain?

SILENCE did not hang over this huge room. Silence punched its way through what sound there was, and finally came to a little group of disconsolate people. The disconsolate people were sitting with their legs over the arms of the folding camp chairs, or they were smoking cigarettes half-way down and stamping on them and looking down at the butts and shaking their heads at the crushed butts. In one way or another they were all saying "Goddamit," and worrying. High above these people, and at an angle, were men in undershirts, not worrying. The men who controlled the lights did not worry much about the people down below; the men with the lights, and the extras, got their dough, and it was up to the disconsolate people to figure out some way to finish the picture. Meanwhile the undershirts and the extras were earning their pay.

A fat man with an Anglo-Irish name and a nose that was strictly from Rivington Street scratched the full growth of hair between his shoulder blades. He shook his head. A skimpy little Irishman shook his. Director, and assistant director.

"I know! Ask Mischa. That's what he gets paid for, writing songs," said the skimpy little Irishman.

"What I was thinking of!" said the director. "Ask 'im."

The little Irishman began calling out, "Mischa, Mischa," and a few moments later one of the extras said to him, "Over there. Over where the card game is going on."

"Why didn't you say so?" said the Irishman. He went over where the card game was going on. "Mischa, we're in a spot," he said.

"Away," said a little man with a waxed mustache. "I bump," he said to another little man at the table. Someone else said, "It's up to you," and then there was more talk of bumping. "This here sounds like 'A Yank at Oxford,'" Mischa said. "Pay me. I go to the head of the river. Now what the hell do you want, jerk?"

"Mischa, we're in a spot," said the little Irishman. "Who?"

"Arch wants to ask you something," said the Irishman.

"I do anything for Arch," said Mischa. "Tell 'im to come over."

"Aw, now, Mischa," said the Irishman.

"Oh, all right. Deal me out," said Mischa.

"Well, anyway, leave some of the matches," said one of the men at the table.

"Sure. I'm in you for like roughly—I'll settle for a deuceroo each. Now what is it, dear? What does Arch want?"

"He—"

"I'll talk to Arch," said Mischa. He got up and went to the director. "What is it, Arch?"

The man with the nose scratched the hair again. "We got all these people here. If we could, I do' know, what's use shooting around people if you got all these people here, but the script don't call—"

"Now listen, Arch," said Mischa. "What do you want and if I can I'll do it. What is it?"

"Music. We're four days behind schedule, and here that means but plenty. If we had something we could fill in, wit' all these people. Like a night-club sequence."

"A night-club sequence," repeated Mischa. "With what you own—you don't want me to write a little number."

"No. I just thought. I don't know what the hell I thought."

"Lit's sit down a minute," said Mischa. "Night club.

Night club. Of course I could *write* something. I better sit down a minute." He sat down, in Arch's folding camp chair, and scratched his chin with one finger. "I know! 'Smile, Brother'!"

" 'Smile, Brother'?"

"Sure," said Mischa. " 'Smile, brother, smile, brother, let's con-grat-u-late each other.' You don't know it? Well, Bing used to sing it with the Rhythm Boys. Eleven years ago. 'It won't be long now.' Bing, Barris—I forget who was with them. You could get it for hay. Buttons. You could get it for buttons."

"Yeah, but we don't want to pay buttons. We don't want to pay anything, Mischa. This, we only want to fill in this night-club sequence."

"Mm. Maybe you own it. Maybe Paramount owns it. But anyway, let me think. I'll play it for you." Mischa, a trumpet player, went to a piano and played it for Arch. Arch liked it. He especially liked it when Mischa and one of the poker players did an imitation of the Rhythm Boys. It was easy to see he wanted it, but it was easy to see he was thinking of the shooting schedule and the budget on this picture. It was so easy to see it that Mischa looked sad, and then Mischa began to think. He asked Arch to wait a minute, and Arch waited more than a minute while Mischa fum-

bled around the unfamiliar piano. Arch went back to
his chair and was almost dozing away when Mischa
yelled out, "Is Wagner in the public domain?"

"I think so," said Arch.

"Send somebody out and find out. Call up. If Wagner is in the public domain we got it."

Arch sent the Irishman to call up and find out if
R. Wagner was in the public domain, and turned back
to Mischa. He said, "But, Mischa, I don't get it. Even
if Wagner is in the public domain what good does
that do us?"

"Arch, for cry sweet sake," said Mischa. "Listen
here. Jevver hear the Fire Music? Well, listen." He
fooled around with the piano, not going above middle
C.

"No," said Arch.

"Well, now listen," said Mischa. He played some
more.

"Oh," said Arch. "Can we do it?"

"We can if Wagner's in the public domain," said
Mischa. "And even if he isn't, for God's sake." Mischa
unbuckled his belt and half turned to Arch. "Geez,
Arch, if I'd of only stayed in school I cudda done the
lyrics too. I'm not gunna wait for that donkey. 'Smile,
brother. . . .' "

Olive

MISS BISHOP had been the hotel's guest six months without having put in or received a call worth listening in on. Within a month of Miss Bishop's checking in, Olive, the day operator, knew all the regulars, outgoing and incoming: the hairdresser in East Forty-seventh Street, the bank downtown, the dry-cleaner, the drugstore, and the Jersey City number. The Jersey City number Olive came to know as Miss Bishop's aunt; a stingy old woman, Olive thought. When Miss Bishop put in a call for the Jersey City number, the call would last ten minutes and sometimes more, but when the aunt's voice asked for Miss Bishop the call stayed within three minutes.

It was always the same. The call would come in at nine or thereabouts, just after Miss Bishop had asked for a waiter to take away the breakfast things: "Olive, will you send someone up please for the breakfast dishes?" An hour later Miss Bishop would appear at the desk and cash a small check, usually ten dollars. Then she would sit and wait for her aunt, who might arrive five minutes later, or might keep Miss Bishop waiting a couple of hours. When the old woman arrived Miss Bishop would go out with her and be gone until three in the afternoon, returning with a few small packages. She would stop at the news-stand and Charlie would hand her the *Sun,* and she would sit reading it in the chair she preferred, in a corner of the small lobby. She would be reading five or ten minutes and Colonel Browder would join her.

Colonel Browder was easily thirty years older than Miss Bishop, but they got along very well together. Miss Bishop never smoked unless Colonel Browder was with her—at least not in the lobby or any of the public part of the hotel. As far as Olive knew, Miss Bishop may have smoked her head off in her room. She must have done something in her room, she spent so much time there.

The Colonel and Miss Bishop were the only guests in the hotel to take tea, and it was understood that the tea and cinnamon toast were to be put on the Colonel's monthly bill without its being presented to him each afternoon.

It was easy to see that the Colonel welcomed the arrival of Miss Bishop at the hotel. When she first came he had been a widower three months and everyone had got used to not having Mrs. Browder around. Her absence made a difference: there was no one to go around complaining of dusty chairs and frequently non-existent cockroaches in the corner nearest the dining-room. For a while the hotel staff missed Mrs. Browder because it was so pleasant without her belly-aching around; and then when the staff had become accustomed to her not being there the Colonel began to miss her. He went around, as Semple, the day clerk, said, like a chicken with its head cut off. When Mrs. Browder died everyone said it was a good thing for the Colonel, and he seemed to think so at first, but that was because he had things to do the first few weeks after her death. When those things had been attended to was when he began to go around like a chicken with its head cut off. Then Miss Bishop arrived and Mr. McLoughlin, the manager, introduced the Colonel to her and they became friends.

The Colonel had given up his parlor-bedroom-bath when Mrs. Browder passed on, and at the time of the change Olive thought to herself that it didn't make much difference in her young life; the only time the Colonel ever used his phone was to ask for the correct time by her clock, and not by the Meridian number. The Colonel sometimes told Olive the telephone was

a waste as far as he was concerned. Too much tele-
phoning. People ought to walk more and use their
legs. He said it was just as easy to walk a block or two
for whatever you wanted as to telephone. Olive did
not reply that she thought he was crazy, which was her
first thought, or that she knew he used the nickel coin-
box in the rear of the dining-room. With these old
babies that lived in the hotel you had to keep a civil
tongue in your head.

But after Miss Bishop and the Colonel had pretty
well established their tea-time as one of the customs
of the hotel Olive began to notice that the Colonel was
using his phone, and for outside calls. The little matters that took him either on short walks or to the nickel
coin-box, he was beginning to take care of from his
room, with calls which cost him a dime apiece. Olive
thought about this a long time before she saw what it
meant—that the Colonel liked to stay around the hotel
as much as possible, or rather to leave it as little as
possible; and the reason he did not use the five-cent
pay station was that he did not want Miss Bishop to
see him chiseling. This, and the standing order for tea,
which was fifteen dollars a month extra on his bill, convinced Olive that the old boy was going for Bishop.
And she was at least thirty years his junior. Bishop was

around thirty-six, giving her a break, and the Colonel was what you might call a well-preserved seventy.

When Olive noticed the Colonel taking an interest in Miss Bishop she began to watch for something big to happen, and then when nothing big happened she kept her eye open for little things. The Colonel always gave Olive five dollars for Christmas—five for her, and five apiece for the other operators, which was the biggest present the operators got. But this did not make Olive warm up to the Colonel. Without doing anything to show it, the Colonel managed to give the impression that he thought talking to telephone operators was beneath him. You could see it in other things: he would talk to Henry, the head waiter, by the hour, or to Tommy Bond, the night clerk. But he would not waste much time with McLoughlin and he hardly ever said a word to any of the bellboys. In other words, a snob. Tommy Bond had gone to a school named Andover and a year to Yale College before the depression got him; Henry (who was not so snobbish that he would not reach for Olive whenever he got a chance), he would listen while the Colonel talked about the wines which he seldom bought. Olive knew McLoughlin noticed it, too. "As long as they pay their bills that's all I'm innarested in. I don't care if they think I'm the dirt under their feet as long as they get it up the first of the month," McLoughlin would say. Olive did not feel the same way about it. Other people thought she was plenty all right. Tommy Bond thought so. Tommy Bond would be getting ready to leave when Olive came to work in the morning, and he always had a few words to say of a kidding nature, not too personal, but Olive knew by the way a man looked at you how he felt about you. She knew Tommy preferred her to Bishop, for instance.

But even that was not satisfactory to Olive. She wondered why it had not occurred to her before, but thinking about how Tommy liked her, she resented it. She resented being liked by the men around the place and not by the women—Miss Bishop now, and Mrs. Browder before. Sex got into it when it was a case of a kid like Tommy Bond liking you. A kid like Tommy liked you irregardless. Telephone operator or society débutante, when a kid like Tommy liked you he didn't care who you were, because what made the difference was sex. Whereas with the Colonel, sex did not enter into the consideration. With Miss Bishop the same. She was a woman, so there was no sex to confuse the issue. Therefore, when Bishop and the Colonel did not like her, that meant it was because they were snobbish about her. What the hell right did they have to be snobbish about her? She was as good as they were any day. She earned her own living and she had good morals.

In regard to her likes and dislikes, Olive never did anything about them until something happened that made her express approval or disapproval, hatred or love. If she liked someone she did not do anything about it until the name of the party came up in a way that led to Olive's coming right out and saying she liked So-and-so; and if underneath she hated someone, it stayed underneath until the occasion when she would get on record as hating them. The occasion when she expressed her feelings about the Colonel and Miss Bishop came fairly soon after she had made up her mind about them.

Melba, the relief operator, came on one afternoon as Olive was quitting for the day, and she made some crack about the Colonel and Miss Bishop. The crack was something unimportant, like: "Mm. The young love birds are having their tea." It was unusual because Melba seldom said anything about the guests, but this day she must have got out of the wrong side of the bed or something.

Olive looked over to the corner of the lobby where

the two were conversing. "Yeah," said Olive. "What is that, anyway? That Bishop. And him. It's enough to make you sick to your stomach, watching them."

"Why, what do they do?" said Melba, who was a little surprised that a casual remark had such effect on Olive.

"What do they do?" said Olive. "Any minute I expect him to give her the business."

"Why, he's too *old*. Isn't he?"

"Too old? He isn't too old to look right through a person worse than any of the bellhops. Didn't you ever notice it?"

"In a way I did," said Melba, who had noticed no such thing, but was not going to tell Olive so.

"Just because he has one foot in the grave don't mean *any*thing," said Olive.

Having thus committed herself, Olive never let up on Miss Bishop and the Colonel. Every time she had a chance she said something against them, always against them as a unit. "Those two," it was. It began to tell in her attitude towards them, and she was curt to Miss Bishop one day over the phone, so much so that Miss Bishop said, "Look here, Olive, don't you talk to me that way."

"If you have any complaints to make you complain to Mr. McLoughlin," said Olive.

"Well, if you're not careful I will," said Miss Bishop.

"Go ahead and see if I care," said Olive. "You or Colonel Browder."

"What about Colonel Browder? What are you talking about?"

"I guess you know," said Olive, and pulled out the cord, disconnecting Miss Bishop. Miss Bishop signaled her to come back, but she made her wait. When she plugged in again and connected Miss Bishop the latter said, "Is this Olive?"

"Yes. Who do you think?"

"Either you apologize or I'll report you to Mr. Mc-Loughlin. I won't have your nasty little insinuations. You're impertinent."

"Go ahead and report me. I don't care."

Miss Bishop did not report Olive, but the next day Olive learned that when the month was up Miss Bishop was leaving the hotel. The day after that she learned, by listening to a conversation, that Miss Bishop was going to live with her aunt in Jersey City temporarily until she found another place. "If you come over here you might as well stay," said the aunt. "I don't see why I should go on paying rent for two places."

In what was left of the month Olive was a little afraid Bishop might go to McLoughlin and snitch on her, but not really afraid. People like Bishop did not get you fired; they were the ones that were afraid, afraid you would get even with them for having you fired.

After Bishop left, Olive looked for some difference on the part of the Colonel. She thought he might be rude to her. But no; his attitude towards her did not change. He didn't notice her. She did hear him tell Semple that for the time being he would go on having tea served, as he expected Miss Bishop to drop in now and then. But she never did.

It Wouldn't Break Your Arm

THE TELEPHONE was there, there was the telephone, and it was easy enough to pick it up and say the number and ask for Dave and be put through to him, and tell him what Claudia had told her. The telephone was not heavy; it wouldn't break your arm to pick it up. There would be no difficulty about reaching Dave; divorced or not divorced, she and Dave were good friends, and Dave always was the soul of consideration, the soul of kindness and thoughtfulness. . . .

She would telephone in just a minute. She lit a cigarette and brought an ash-tray over to the chair. Now what should she say? Should she start out by saying, "I just heard something that I thought you'd want to hear?" No, that was too blunt. Be better to say, "Do you remember hearing me talking about Claudia Howard? From Evanston? She went to school with me." No, that wasn't so good, either. It was sort of presuming, kind of proprietary, a little as though she expected him to go on thinking thoughts with her

the way they had in the old days. So she would have
to give a casual explanation of who Claudia Howard
was. Where you would have to be more explicit would
be in telling how she happened to know Pauline.

Oh, even now she disliked—disliked, hell; hated—
what that name could do to her. Pauline. Pauline
Jeffries. What a common-sounding name that was.
Frances tried to be fair about it, and she knew she was
fair. And still it was a common-sounding name. Now,
more than a year since she had been married, she felt
she was completely unprejudiced about that name, and
all she could think was that it was a common-sounding
name. Two years ago it might have been different.
Two years ago, when Dave spoke the name, Frances
had thought it was common-sounding, but then she
might have been prejudiced. But not now. And she
told herself that she was a little glad to be able to be
so dispassionate and confirm her original opinion about
the sound of the name Pauline Jeffries. And Pauline
Jeffries never had been any more than a name to her.
She never had laid eyes on the woman, never met her.
All she knew was that Pauline Jeffries had been the
love of Dave's life, that's all. When Dave got married,
after he and Frances settled down and his friends began
to come to see them, some of them used to kid Dave

about Pauline. "Well, Dave," they would say, "you
left one broken heart back home. You know, Mrs.
Werner, your husband, gave one of our nicest girls the
air to marry you. I suppose he told you all about
Pauline, though." Not many of them had been as
blunt as that, but that's what they all meant. Then she
had heard from Dave the story of his romance with
Pauline. One of those things. Small town. Two people,
they get thrown together a lot at parties. First thing
you know people have them engaged, and as a matter
of fact, they did get engaged.

Then, after it was out, Dave felt freer to talk about
Pauline. She was a brunette. She was—yes, you could
call her a tall girl. Taller than average. In fact she had
quite a nice figure and people always commented on
her walk. They said with that walk Pauline ought to
be a model, with that walk and that figure, and the
way she wore clothes. But Pauline a model! It was
laughable. No; Pauline was really retiring. Not that
she didn't like people. She loved people. Her house
was practically the headquarters for the whole country
club crowd, or at least the gang Dave traveled with.
And no wonder. Pauline was a natural hostess, and
nothing was ever too much for her. After a dance at
the club they'd all troop back to Pauline's house, and

no matter what time of the night it was, Pauline'd just tell one person to do this, someone else to do that, someone else to do that, and pretty soon breakfast would be in process of preparation. But the scrambled eggs Pauline would do herself. No one could make scrambled eggs like Pauline's, and no one would dispute that. In fact, it was a rare thing in a girl who was so modern as Pauline—well dressed, good sport, good looking, and all that—but the fact of the matter was, Pauline was just about as good a cook as Dave ever knew. Some people, you know, they just seem to have the right touch about food, about cooking, and Pauline was one of those fortunate females. Although unfortunate in some ways, because it meant she'd have to make the scrambled eggs when she'd rather have been out on the sun porch with Dave. But that was all over.

Except that it wasn't all over, and the longer she was married to Dave, the less Frances believed it was all over. And finally she began to believe that it was not over at all. Then one day she could stand it no longer and she asked Dave if Pauline ever came to New York, and before he had had time to think he said yes. She didn't have to ask Dave if he had seen Pauline. She knew. Then there had been the period of his trying to make up for it, and that was the loveliest

time of their marriage, because he seemed to mean it
when he said he loved her, and he seemed to mean it
so much more because he said it against her doubt.
He told her he was afraid of losing her, and that he
would do anything to avoid that. He had got the habit
of loving her, he said. He had put too much into their
marriage to have it break up because of a few lunch
dates with an old girl. And that's all there had been,
he assured her—and she believed him.

But that lovely period ended, too. Weeks later she
found out why, and the reason was that Dave had
heard that Pauline was going to get married. And then
Frances found out something else she always had
known: Dave loved Pauline as he never would love
anyone else. The reason Pauline never would marry
Dave was her fear of his drinking: if he would go on
the wagon for a year she would marry him. "I never
asked him to go on the wagon," Frances reminded
herself. Well, at that point there was no chance of his
going on the wagon, if by a remote chance she had
wanted him to. For when Pauline got married he
would come home tight or plastered or drunk two or
three times a week, and there never was a marriage
that was worth anything while the husband was drunk
and the wife was sober. So Frances decided that when

Dave came home, she would be a little tight herself, so she began to drink cocktails at the accustomed hour, and when Dave would come home, frequently she would be as tight as he. That was all right when he was tight, but when she was tight and he came home sober, that was not so good. He hated to see her through sober eyes when she had had enough to drink to make it noticeable that she had been drinking. He told her she could cut that out. Then he told her she damn sure better cut it out if she knew what was good for her; he wasn't going to stand it, coming home every evening and finding her cock-eyed drunk. So she did cut it out for a while, and then he started again, and this time he was bad, because he would call her things she did not like and would not stand for. But worse than the things he would call her was his repeating his firm conviction that their marriage had been a mistake. The first time he said that she was insulted, but put it down to his drunkenness. It was when he repeated it two or three times, and added that she had kept him from marrying the only girl he ever really loved (although she could not see how she had kept him from anything)—that was when she took up drinking again, and stuck to it just long enough to find out that some other man had arms and a mouth and tenderness and passion and even admiration—admiration most of all— that suited her. That, Dave said, was the last straw.

Well, he had been generous about the money end of it. He was doing all right in business. What's more, he assured her, he liked her. Any time she needed anything he wanted her to promise him she'd come to him first, and if it was humanly possible, he'd do it. And by the same token he hoped she would let him take her out to lunch or dinner, football game, theatre—things like that. Well, that wasn't quite the new start she had begun to hope to make, but he was so generous and all, she had to say yes.

That was it. He was so generous. He wanted to do things for her. She could do this for him. She picked up the telephone and gave his number.

"Dave? Fran. Dave, I was just talking to an old friend of mine. Oh, you wouldn't know her, Dave, but she told me something I thought you might like to hear. This girl lives in Evanston, and—yes, she knows her. Now wait till I tell you. This girl saw your picture on my dresser, and she said, 'Why, I've seen his picture lots of times. Pauline Rockwell, a girl out in Evanston, she has this same picture in her bedroom,

and we always thought it was her brother.' Imagine
a thing like that, Dave? That must mean your old love
isn't getting along so well with her husband or she
wouldn't keep your picture on her chiffonier. I just
thought that would amuse you."

My Girls

FOR SOME reason—oh, why? oh, why anything?—
Mrs. Cole had made herself sit with her back to
the windows. She knew it was partly because she did
not want to see the roadster coming up the street. But
why not? Well, some day a hundred years from now
she might be able to answer that question. Now it made
no difference. The reason made no difference in the
world. All she knew was that she had made herself sit
so that she could not see the street, and thus it was that
the first she knew Jane was home was when she heard
the gravel crunching in the drive. Then the sound of
the racing engine, which Jane always made before
switching off the ignition. Then the screen door, and
two heeltaps on the hardwood floor before Jane's feet
reached the hall rug. All sounds that filled Mrs. Cole
with the mysterious fear that is like the fear just before
going into the doctor's inner office.

"Jane," she said.

"Hello," Jane called from the hall.

"Jane, will you come here? Please? I want to talk to you."

"In a minute."

"No, now, please."

"Mother, I'd really *like* to go upstairs, *eef* you don't mind."

"All right, but please——"

"All *right!*" said Jane. "What difference can two *minutes* . . ." Her voice died down.

Mrs. Cole waited, and then there were Jane's deliberate footsteps on the stairs, and then she was standing in the room, for a fraction of a second deciding which chair to sit in. "What is it? It must be terribly important."

Mrs. Cole looked at her daughter. Yes, she probably should have known. *Could* have known. But thought became anger, and Mrs. Cole began to breathe deeply. She stared at her daughter.

"Well?" said Jane.

"You've——done——everything, haven't you?"

"Oh, now really. What is this, anyway? *What* have I done?"

"I say, you've done everything. Haven't you?"

"I heard you say it. First time. Be a little more specific. *What* everything?"

"Who is a boy named Roddy?"

"Oh."

"Yes. Oh."

"I see. I suppose Laura Wilton's been over here in my absence."

"I haven't seen Laura Wilton," said Mrs. Cole.

"You must have. No one else here knows I know this boy." Then: "Oh, *no! Oh,* no. You wouldn't open, you wouldn't open a letter. Oh, oh. You did. Oh, what disgusting— Dis*gus*ting." Jane stood up.

"*Sit* down. I want to have this out with you before your father comes home."

"I'd rather not be in the same room with you."

"Well, you'll just have to. Or perhaps you'd rather have your father here, too."

"I suppose you've showed him the letter."

"No, I haven't. I want to know all about this. Who is this boy?"

"What good will it do you to know that? I won't tell you anything about him."

"I know quite a little about him right this minute. And I know quite a lot about you."

"Well, aren't you pleased with yourself? Especially the way you found out. Now may I have the letter?

Maybe you'd like to know I came home early because I was expecting a letter."

"No letter came. This one was post-marked March twenty-eighth." Mrs. Cole paused. "I think it was the twenty-eighth. It could have been the twenty-sixth or the twenty-ninth."

"That's funny. That's really funny. That was the first letter he ever wrote me. That's why I kept it. You should have seen some of the others, if you liked that so much. How did you happen to find this one?"

"I thought I'd surprise you. I knew you were having trouble with your radio, so I sent for the repair man, and when he came he said he'd have to take it away with him, and that's how I found this letter."

"But that doesn't explain how you happened to read it."

"I won't try to explain that."

"No, dear. You can't. You never can, as long as you live. Well, what are you going to do? Have me put in a home for delinquent girls or something?"

"Hiding a letter in a radio."

"It wasn't a very good place, was it? Well, I still say, what are you going to do? Besides tell Father."

"That's just it. You know I couldn't."

"Oh-ho. You could do anything," said Jane. "But I

wonder what he'll think when you tell him how you found out. He'll love that. It's the kind of thing that he'd die rather than do. Die."

"Well, we'll have to take this up again, because there he is now."

Neither the mother nor her daughter could come to a decision about leaving the room, and then there was Mr. Cole, hair in disarray from the wind, a thick knitted wool scarf sticking out from under his upturned coat collar, two tennis racquets under his arm, white flannels turned up at the cuffs, shoes stained from an En-Tout-Cas court. He was smiling.

"I beat Harry Young in straight sets," he said. "Seven-five, six-two. Six-*two*. And I've never beaten him before in my life. Oh, was he burned up! And the worst loser." Mr. Cole dropped into a chair. "He was feeling very cocky, so he said before we started, 'Jim, I'll give you a break. I'll give you three games a set.' Well, of course he's usually been giving me one game. And beating me. Maybe once in a while I'll take a seven-fiver, but I've never beaten him; that is, I've never left the court a winner. But today, I don't know, I was so damn mad when the so-and-so gave me three games a set, I said, 'For how much?' He said, 'Oh, the usual five bucks.' 'Make it ten,' I said. He laughed.

Didn't want to take my money. That kind of thing. By the way, Janie, ring for Joseph, will you, please? I feel a Tom Collins coming on."

Jane reached behind her and pushed a button.

"I—" Mr. Cole began. "Say, what's the matter? Have my girls been battling again? What is it this time?"

Mrs. Cole said nothing. Jane said nothing. Then Mrs. Cole stood up. "You'll have to excuse me, please," she said, and went up the stairs.

"Oh, now, what's the matter? You tell me, Janie? . . . Uh, Joseph, I'd like a Tom Collins. Janie, how about something for you?"

"No, thanks."

"Yes, sir," said Joseph, and went out. Jane left too. She ran up the stairs and went to her mother's room.

"Mother." Her mother was lying on the bed.

"What?" said Mrs. Cole.

"Mother, can't we tell him it's about money, or something?"

Mrs. Cole put her handkerchief to her eyes. "Yes, we'll have to. Oh, come here. Janie."

No Sooner Said

THE LAST drawer of the file coasted back on its ball bearings and settled in place with a slight thump. Miss Ross pushed the button lock and turned the key, which locked all the drawers in the file at one turn. She went to her desk and took out her purse and a folded towel. Mr. Jay stared straight ahead, holding his hand to his forehead like an Indian shading his eyes from the sun, and at the same time resting his head in that hand. He heard Miss Ross's footsteps going down the hall, and a few minutes later he heard her coming back. She put her purse on the desk, folded the towel again and put it in the drawer of the desk, and went to the water-cooler, to one side of which was a mirror, to the other side a clothes tree. There were two hats on the clothes tree—Miss Ross's was a Juliet cap, white, but to make it modern there was a two-inch thick woolen pigtail in the middle; and the other hat was Mr. Jay's, a three-dollar straw number with a plain black band. Reaching for her cap, Miss Ross, more concerned with her face in the mirror, knocked Mr. Jay's hat to the floor. It gave forth a couple of hollow sounds before settling flat.

"Oh, I beg your pardon! I knocked your hat off."

"That's all right," said Mr. Jay. "That hat's had plenty of knocking around."

"But look what I *did*. It's chipped."

"No, you didn't do that. That was there before."

"Are you positive? No. There, right there." She stooped over a second time, this time picking up a fragment of straw hat. "Here's a piece of straw, so I must have. I must of done it. How much was it?"

"Oh. A little chip off it? What's that? I've got my money's worth out of that lid."

"No, but I think in view of the fact that it was my carelessness plus my vanity. If I hadn't been so vain as to look at myself in the mirror instead of paying attention to what I was doing. Let me pay *part* of a new hat. I'd really feel much better about the whole matter."

"Nope. No thanks. I wouldn't think of it, Miss Ross."

"Well, if you want to be gall*ant*, Mr. Jay. But I *am* very sorry. Why? What are you smiling about?"

"I was just thinking, here we've been in the same office—you came here right after the first of the year—

and this is the first time we ever had any conversation outside of business."

"Yes, that's correct," said Miss Ross.

"Go on."

"What do you mean, go on?"

"Well, there was something in the way you said that that made me think you were going to say something else."

"Maybe I was, or at least thinking something else. But perhaps I better not."

"Go ahead."

"Well, frankly, Mr. Jay, the people in this office don't seem over-enthusiastic about me, as a person."

"Why, Miss *Ross?* I happen to know from Mr. Mc-Dowell himself, he happened to say the other day, he said, 'That Ross girl gets more work done than any other girl in the office,' and he mentioned, he said about how you caught on so quickly. He said you have a positively photographic memory. You know—being able to remember everything on one of those cards, just from one look."

"Oh, that. That's a minor accomplishment. I could always do that. When I went to Evander, I never had to study hard. That's just a thing that's born in you."

"Have a cigarette?"

"Yes, thank you. I guess it's all right after hours."

"Yes, the least they can do is let us smoke if they make us work overtime. Here, I'll light it for you."

"Thank you." She took off her hat again and ruffled her hair, and sat on top of a desk. "How long have you been here, Mr. Jay?"

"Seven and a half years."

"I see you're a member of Phi Beta Kappa."

"Oh, yes. For what it's worth. I don't know why I wear the damn thing. I guess it's the only thing that makes my wife give me credit for having any brains."

"Oh, are you married?"

"Don't I look it? I'll be married eleven years next October. We have two children, two girls. One just eight and the other going on five."

"Oh, really?"

"Yes, two little girls. What about you? Are you married?"

"Not me. I've never been specially urged."

"I don't believe that."

"Well, it's sad but true, Mr. Jay. Oh, I know a lot of young dopes, they get hot pants—I beg your pardon."

Mr. Jay laughed. "Don't tell *me*. *I* know."

"Oh, but think of me using an expression like that! I mean, the first time."

"Well, what the hell, it's the truth, isn't it? It's true, and they want to get married on twenty-five dollars a week. By God, if my girls want to get married, they'll have to bring around a couple of men that can support them. Of course by the time they're ready to get married, maybe there won't be any marriage."

"You sound like my brother. Are you a Communist?"

"Communist? Me? That's a lifework. To be a member of the party—"

"I know. I get it from Mortie all the time. His idea of Utopia would be an income of, say, a hundred bucks a week so he could go around and agitate. Agitate. He's right, of course, but it just doesn't work out that way."

"Well, I wish him luck. But if he's sincere, you tell him not to get married."

"Apropos of marriage, what made you think I might be?"

"Well, we had a girl here, the girl that had your job before you came, and none of us knew she was married, but about two or three months after she quit she had a baby, and her husband didn't even have a job. Maybe you heard the other girls mention her. Miss Gallon."

"No, I never heard of her. The other girls! I've been here since January and there isn't one of them ever so much as asked me to have lunch with her. I don't mean pay for it; I just mean have it together, Dutch. What's the matter with me?"

"You're too pretty."

"No, it isn't that. I know what it is, all right. Miss Kelly. I've seen her letters. The worst speller I ever saw, but I guess I know how she holds her position."

"I guess we all do, more or less."

"Yes. And that Simpson dame. It's a very personal thing, but somebody oughta give her a bath. Her *neck* is dirty. And that dope that has the desk next to mine. Schmidt. Huh. The others I don't come in contact with so very much. Oh, I can't wait to get out of this place. I've been looking for another position for weeks. But don't say anything, Mr. Jay."

"Certainly not."

"This is the first human conversation I've had since I came here. Well—in a way. It depends on what you call human."

"I know what you mean."

"No, you don't. You couldn't possibly. The conversation I have reference to didn't take place in the office."

"But I'll bet I know," said Mr. Jay.

"No, you don't."

"Was it with Mr. McDowell?"

"Yes. How did you know?" said Miss Ross.

"I know the signs. First he waits till Kelly goes out to lunch, and then he comes out and looks around the office and pretends he picks a girl at random. Then he says, 'Uh, Miss Ross, can you take dictation?' And of course you say you can, and he says he has a letter he wants to get off right away. Remember?"

"*Do* I!"

"Then the next sign is when he tells me what a good worker you are. Listen, I've been here over seven years."

"Well, all I can say is I'm glad I started looking for another job."

"Did he accidentally take you home?"

"About as accidental as—as if he sent me a memo saying, 'Be in the car or else,' " she said.

"Another cigarette?"

"No, thanks. I have to be going."

"Will you do me a favor?"

"Of course."

"Don't quit this job. I mean before you quit, let me know. Sometimes I get fed up here, too."

"Why? The girls making passes at you, Mr. Jay? Oh, I'm sorry I said that, really I am."

"It's all right." There was a silence.

"Why don't you do the rest of that tomorrow? Do you live uptown?"

"All the *way* uptown," said Mr. Jay.

"Well—do you want to walk part of the way? I feel like walking."

"No sooner said than done," said Mr. Jay.

Invite

Dear Betty:

I debated within myself a long time whether to call you Betty, not that I didn't call you Betty last summer and you me Harry, but as neither of us kept our promise to write I was not sure whether we should return to the formal basis. However I have a feeling that having gone through those stirring times in London together I suppose we will never forget them and I know that for my part whenever I think of London in 1938 and those times I will always think of Betty.

Well, it did not turn out the way we feared and for that let us be grateful. Not that I was not disappointed in Chamberlain but I suppose it is better to have peace than war no matter how much it cost England in prestige. I know for my part I prefer to be back here in college enjoying the life than in uniform standing in a muddy trench, waiting for the given signal to go "over the top" and kill my fellow man, who, just because he happens to be a German is still my fellow man. I suppose I am a pacifist at heart although I would naturally go to war and lay down my life if this country were ever invaded and I imagine you would feel the same way if you were a man.

Well, how are you liking it at Smith? I hope better than you did freshman year. Remember I told you in London how you would like it better when you were a sophomore? Personally I did not mind freshman year so much. I made a lot of new acquaintances and friends freshman year and although some of them have not lasted, still some of them have, and now that I am an upperclassman I am satisfied to have my own circle of friends, some of them in the fraternity but some not. I am not narrow about fraternity stuff. Just because a fellow I liked happened to go Phi Psi and I went Delt does not mean that I have to hate him. That stuff went out years ago. In fact my father was not a Delt. When he was here he was a Tau Phi Alpha, which was then a local and is now national, S. A. E. When I came here he told me I could go anything I please. "Any crowd that will have you," he said humorously. I think that is the right attitude and if my son comes here he can go any fraternity he wants, preferably Delt because we have always had a good well-rounded house, not too many athletes and not too many honor students and not too many playboys. Three years ago we won the Heffelberger Cup, emblematic of having the highest scholastic average of any fraternity house on the campus, and last year we had captain of baseball, three Phi Betes, two guys that just missed Phi Bete, chairman of the Junior Prom, and also the chapter won the touch football championship and also were runners-up in interfraternity tennis. So you see we have a well-rounded house with varied interests. We also have some wealthy alumni. At all our big football games you ought to see the Lincolns and Cadillacs parked in the driveway. One of the alumni from Lake Forest has a Rolls but he never brings it to the games.

Well, I guess all this fraternity stuff doesn't mean very much to you, being an Eastern girl, but I just thought I would tell you a few things as I wanted to ask you if you could come out here for Junior Prom, as my guest. I know what you will think, too far. Well, it is pretty far but not if you come by plane. If you flew to Chicago I could meet you there in my car and it is only a pleasant drive from Chicago. We would be here in plenty of time for the tea dance Friday afternoon. (I hope your folks have no objection to flying.) As to where you would stay while here you would stay at the Kappa house (Kappa Kappa Gamma). That is the best sorority on the campus and is just around the corner literally from our house. We and the Kappas have an arrangement that the men the Kappas bring to Prom stay at our house and the women we bring stay at the Kappa house. You would like the Kappas. A lot of them get their clothes in the East and have their own cars and have more members of the Junior League than any other sorority. Some of the other sororities call the Kappas a hi-hat crowd but I don't think that is fair. Several times during the year we have joint dances, informals, with the Kappas and you would not want to meet a nicer crowd. Easterners get a wrong idea of the girls out here. One Kappa, Marge Holt by name, spends practically all her time in the "21" Club when she is in New York and knows Ted Husing. She and I were the only ones who could really do the Lambeth Walk as she was also in London last summer before you got there. She is anxious to meet you as I have told her all about you. I told her you saved my life in London. If it hadn't been for you I probably would have been bored to death in spite of all the stirring times. Her mother and father were both born in Brooklyn but Marge was born in Fort Wayne and is a member of the Fort Wayne Junior League. She is half engaged to a Psi U from Michigan, but if you come out don't say anything about that as it is unofficial.

She and I used to see a lot of each other freshman and sophomore year but before she went abroad she went up to northern Michigan for a week and fell in love with Bud. I don't remember his last name. I must have been very enthusiastic about you because she said to me the other night, "Harry, isn't it wonderful how things turn out?" She and I were never really in love and she meant it was wonderful how we could be on the friendship basis again, although I did not infer to her that you were in love with me. However, she seemed to think I was in love with you, just from things I said, and perhaps she knows me better than I know myself. She is a wise old girl, is our Marge, despite a reputation for being frivolous. She hardly ever cracks a book but if she did she would easily have straight A's but she would rather just manage to stay in college and have a whirl than miss the fun and be a good student. She says she expects to get married twice! I wonder how Bud would like that if he heard it. She knows she could be good at anything she tried but she says what is the use of her taking a job away from some girl that really needs it. Her folks have plenty of money so I suppose she is right. Sometimes she is very deep.

Well, how's about it? You have plenty of time to think it over and I wish you would let me know the minute you decide. You could be back in Northampton Sunday night I believe. They are trying very hard to get Tommy Dorsey for Prom. It will be announced next week. The program is tea dances Friday afternoon and joint dinner at our house (Kappas and their guests and our guests and we). There will be a basketball game that night but we can miss that as it is only a freshman game. There is also a Glee Club concert before Prom and that may be good. Then Prom until four and then breakfast party at the Kappa house. The next day (Saturday) there is nothing special doing till the tea dances when every house has open house and then Buffet supper at the Kappa house. After that the 'varsity basketball game and after the game informal dancing at the gym. It has to be informal as there is a faculty rule that dancing has to end at 12 midnight Saturday night. You would only have to bring one evening dress that is for Prom. If you could stay over Sunday afternoon and evening there is a roadhouse about twenty miles from here that used to be a country club and is very nice. We usually go there Sunday afternoon when we have dates. It is just a pleasant drive and if you have never seen the farming country out here it might prove interesting to an Easterner.

Well, I have sketched the Prom week-end for you

and I hope it sounds interesting. If you would come it would be the first time one of our crowd has had a girl from so far East, and we would go to town showing you a good time. Last year one girl came from Pittsburgh but she was plastered practically all the time she was here, not that there is any objection to drinking but this girl made herself objectionable and was suspected of stealing a diamond wrist watch from one of the girls over at Kappa. She was definitely not the type girl we or the Kappas prefer to have.

So come on and let us show you that all the fun is not at Yale and Princeton and those places. Also we can talk about the stirring times we had in London which will prove interesting to those who were not there.

I have a lot of things I want to talk about in person but that will have to wait. Well, as they say in dear old London, cheerio.

From

"CHAMBERLAIN"

P.S.: If you could wire me this week it would be so much the better.

All the Girls He Wanted

THEY were wrong about giving yourself something
to do and making yourself do it. They were just
as wrong about that as they were about everything else.
Even Elise was wrong. Even Elise? Wronger than the
rest of them. She knew enough to make her worse than
anyone else. Elise would be around, trying to be help-
ful, trying to understand and be understanding, saying,
"We must do this, we must do that. You can come to
New York with me. You can do this, you can do that."
Elise— But no use picking flaws with Elise. Obviously
Elise had not read the papers, or she would have been
calling up hours ago. Frances persisted in thinking
about Elise. This is what she would say over the telephone: "Darling, my poor darling, I just heard (or
read) (or just this minute found out). I'm coming
right over." She would be very cagey about what she
said on the telephone. Elise was very cagey. Years of
living in the country, with party lines, had made her
distrust the telephone. Elise would write anything in
a telegram, because it was her theory that the people

at the Western Union never actually read the words. In fact she thought they probably hated the words, all words, because they got so tired of them. Elise could, and had, built up a character, a Western Union clerk who just wanted to be somewhere where there wasn't a word, not a single word. . . . You could say to Elise: "But if they don't read telegrams, how is it they put one star on one kind, and two stars on a more important kind, and so on?" "Oh, well, they read them, but they don't associate the message with the people who send them or receive them." But she would not say so much as "stocking" or "not feeling well" over the telephone, because some lineman, some operator, would hear her and think in terms of taking liberties. And so she would not say anything over the telephone when she read about Cliff. She would not even mention Cliff by name, or the incident. She would just say: "I just heard. I'm coming right over." And make it worse than anything could be. Still, Elise knew, and she was the only one who did know.

A part of Frances closer to the surface said, "Don't go on pretending to dust things. You have been dusting this piano long enough. Sit down."

She sat down, glad to relinquish her hold on the dustcloth, which was ugly to the touch. She crossed her

feet and contemplated her ankles and legs. "If I were
an English girl, I would say that I had a ladder in my
stocking." She had noticed that there was a sale of
stockings at Bloom's. A dollar sixty-nine. Well, they'd
better be good this time. The last time she'd bought
stockings at Bloom's, at a sale, they were no damn good
whatever. She had noticed this advertisement this
morning, not an hour ago, when she first picked up the
paper. Although as a matter of fact she had not picked
up the paper. The paper was lying on the dining-room
table, where Ralph had left it after breakfast, and she
had turned the pages, but she had not picked it up. It
was funny Ralph hadn't said anything when he read
the front page. No, it wasn't funny. She had not been
in the dining-room when Ralph appeared for breakfast.
She had been upstairs, being slightly ill. And Ralph
was not one to call upstairs with a piece of news about
Cliff Kizer. If she had been sitting across the table from
Ralph he would have said: "Say, here's something.
Cliff Kizer's dead. 'S car went over the Lincoln Street
bridge. Four o'clock this morning. Huh. I wonder
where *he* was coming from. Well, that's tough. He
was a pretty nice guy. Talking to him only the other
night." And so on. That's the way Ralph would receive
the news, and Frances was glad she had not been there.

It was better to find it out the way she did: with her growing regularity she had been sick, had come downstairs, had gone to the dining-room, had *not* picked up the paper, had read Bloom's ads, and then had turned over to the front page and there it was, a one-column picture of Cliff with his hair parted in the middle. It must have been taken ten years ago, when he was in University School, because from the little you could see, he seemed to be wearing a football shirt. She hadn't noticed that his neck was pretty thick, but there it was. Where the sweater ended, where his neck began, he was wider than at any point on his head. He must have outgrown that. Just as he outgrew football. He never played football at college, she happened to know.

Kizer, junior, killed in four A.M. Lincoln Avenue auto drop. She knew the wording by heart, remembered which words were in the top line, which in the bottom. She knew the statistics of the accident; the number of feet from the bridge to the railroad, the condition of the car, the name of the doctor who pronounced him dead. They had his age wrong: he was twenty-seven, not thirty. Ah, what did all that matter? He was dead, wasn't he? They'd killed him. They had fractured his skull, broken several ribs, broken both legs, bunged him up so that he died before the arrival of the St. Mary's Hospital ambulance. She wondered what beast had thought to put in the newspaper article ". . . that the car did not catch fire was a mystery to police." Could they be hinting that he had committed suicide? What else could they mean? And why should he commit suicide? If anyone had everything, he had. A nice father and mother, plenty of money, good looks, all the girls he—all the girls he wanted.

All the girls he wanted, and he never even thought of wanting me, she said. Once he had kissed her, it was true. Once, and then he was pretty drunk, and his manner toward her never had changed, which certainly proved that he did not remember it. Four years ago, at the Charity Ball. Her own crowd, like every other crowd in town, had taken a room at the hotel, where they could do their semi-private drinking, and he had wandered in and said: "Hello, Frances."

"Hello, Cliff," she had said.

"You want a drink? Have a drink with me?"

"All right," she said. And then he had to explain that he had not brought his liquor with him. Down the hall in his room. And she had said it was all right, there was plenty to drink here. And they'd had a drink.

"Why you alone?" he said. "Why you all alone here?"

"I didn't feel like dancing," she said. No, she hadn't said that. She had said: "The others went down to dance." That was it, because he said: "But you didn't. You stayed here to drink with me? Is that it?"

And she had said: "That's it."

"I never see you any more since you got married," he had said, after looking at his glass. "How do you like married, being married?"

"I like it fine," she had said.

"Ralph treat you all right? He's a nice fellow. A little dull, a little bit dull, just a little bit on the dull side. A little bit on the dull side, I would say, but a nice fellow regardless. Salt of the earth if ever I heard one. If ever I saw one. Ralph is the salt of the earth. You don't care if I say he's dull? You don't mind? You're not angry with me?"

"No, I guess not," she had said.

"Well, that's fine, because I like you, Frances. I always like you. Always did and always will. If you'd of been a little older, three years older, I'd a had a love affair with you and married you when I was seventeen. But you were too young. You're a pretty girl, Frances. You know what I always said about you?"

"No."

"I tell you. I always said Frances Denby, when she

grows up she's gonna be the prettiest girl in this town. That's exactly what I said about you. And I was right. Wasn't I right? Sure. Don't be modest. Prettiest girl in the whole town. United States. How old are you, Frances?"

"Twenty."

"Twenty. Just think. Twenty years old and married. That's very young, Frances. You married very young. Oh, well, in India do you know how old they are when they get married? Six years old. Six years old. Do you know why? You know why? Well, maybe I better not tell you that. I don't know you very well, but I could if I wanted to. I could tell you why they get married in India when they're six years old. But I won't. It's something about the climate, but I won't tell you what it does to girls in that climate. I don't know you well enough, Frances. But I do say this, Frances. You're the prettiest girl in town. In the United States, I mean. United States almighty! Am I drunk! United States almighty!"

And then he had looked at her and smiled, and came over to the bed, where she was sitting, and kissed her. It was a single long kiss, and when it began she still had her drink in her hand. But she put it on the floor, partly to keep from spilling it, partly to enable her to put her arm around Cliff. He did not paw her, except a very little, and that was when she put her hand under his coat, between his shoulder-blades. She was still thinking that it was not at all like what she expected, when he was suddenly gone, staggering down the hall. Lovely. She had stayed there awhile, presently lighting a cigarette and sipping her drink, and as she lay there she kept thinking about how they could have gone somewhere and been by themselves. She kept thinking plans, long after he had gone.

For a year after that she had thought about him, with no disloyalty in her heart. She loved Ralph, enjoyed staying with him, hated him, sometimes was a little jealous when he danced too often with the same girl at parties, but he was her husband, her life. Cliff wasn't anything. Not her husband, not her life, not her lover, not her love. She was glad that the Kizers were so rich and belonged to a different country club. She wanted it that way. She wanted it so that if she ever saw Cliff again and he wanted to kiss her, it would be just like taking it up where they had left off in the hotel. And if she ever had really seen him, she was completely ready to go on. All he had to do was say the word. Or not even say the word! See her alone sometime, and she would go anywhere with him. She would meet him in Chicago, go to a roadhouse, steal away from everyone at the Charity Ball, or go to his apartment (or the apartment people said he had), just so long as no one would find out. If she could be sure of that, she would go anywhere. And that's not asking too much, she knew.

But then a day came when this thinking about him surprised her by getting out of control. For no reason she suddenly wanted him and no one else. It's what I get, she told herself, for having these thoughts about him all this time. Whatever it was, she almost telephoned him, but didn't. She thought of having a party just so she could invite him, but didn't. There was nothing she could do, and she knew it. And that day Elise had dropped in and she had told Elise.

She first had to explain to Elise that there was no more to the affair than just that single long kiss. "If there was more I'd tell you," she said.

"No, you wouldn't," said Elise.

"No, I suppose you're right. I probably wouldn't. But you don't think I'm awful to feel this way about him, do you?"

"Not at all. If he ever kissed me I'd feel that way myself."

"But it wasn't only because he kissed me," said

Frances. "I was crazy about him when I was a little girl."

"Oh, yes," said Elise. "I vaguely remember that. You went to dancing school with him. Wasn't that it?"

"Yes, for a little while. He was so much older in those days, and he stopped going to dancing school right after I started."

"Mm-hmm. Well, what are you going to do about it?" said Elise.

"Nothing, of course. What can I do about it? He never notices me. Oh, he says hello if he sees me downtown, but he never goes to parties that we go to. What can I do? I just had to tell you. Do you mind?"

"No, why should I? It's a good thing to get it out of your system. Honest confession is good for the soul. Just as long as this doesn't affect your relationship with Ralph. You don't want to do anything foolish, darling."

"Oh, I won't," she said.

"All right. But I want you to promise me not to. You said awhile ago you were thinking of having a party and getting Ralph to ask him to come. Don't do anything like that, promise me?"

"I promise," said Frances. "That would be foolish, wouldn't it?"

"It certainly would. Ralph would be suspicious right away. Believe me, Frances, I know. I'm a lot older than you, and I know about such things."

"Yes, you're right," said Frances. And Elise was right, and she did know. It was at times like that that you remembered about Elise; thirty, and divorced, living alone, with a chance to think things out. Elise was a brave girl and a good friend. Frances leaned on her in the intervening years, even though she did not talk much about Cliff.

Now, sitting here, she found she could count the times she had talked to Elise about Cliff. Not more than twice a year, actually. She found herself thinking that in a thing like this, if one good friend merely knows about how you feel, it isn't necessary to talk much about it. The friend knows, and you know. She knew that the moment Elise heard, she would telephone. Elise, the one person in God's world who had any idea of the foolish little secret. She suddenly wanted to talk to Elise, because Elise had been sympathetic. Indeed, of the few times they actually had spoken of Cliff, now that she thought back on them Frances recalled that half the time it was Elise who would say: "By the way, still feel the same way about

Cliff Kizer?" And Frances would say yes, that it was no better and no worse, that she would still go away with him—or would have up to four months ago, when she decided to have a baby and now was going to have one. But the baby was nothing today. This was Cliff's day, and anyway, the baby would not even be a baby for a dreary long time to come. This was Cliff's day, the day of his death, the day he went smashing through a railing and smashing down on the railroad tracks. They had broken his bones and torn his skin, smashed his teeth and made him all terrible and bloody. They had taken life out of him and left him there in a car that did not catch fire. They—God—had not even burned him up with fire, but had left his terrible broken body for anyone to see. Frances hugged herself, drew her arms close to herself. There was more of him in her own arms, that she could feel against her body, than there was at the hospital, or the undertaker's, or wherever they had taken him. The telephone screamed.

Again a change came over her on the way to the telephone, and more than anything in the world she hoped it was not Elise. But she could not let it ring. It might not be Elise.

"Hello," she said.

"Hello, darling." It was Ralph. "Listen, did you see the paper? About Cliff Kizer?"

"Yes. I just read it a few minutes ago. Isn't it awful?"

"It's worse than you think," he said. "Have you talked to anybody about it?"

"No, why?"

"Well, you'd better take the car and go out to Elise's."

"Elise's? You mean Elise Dow?" she said.

"Yes. Now listen, get this. You're not supposed to know it, but Elise tried to kill herself when she heard about Cliff."

"Elise? Why, she didn't know him."

"Well, she did. She was having an affair with him, apparently."

"Where did you hear this? I don't believe it."

"Now don't be so damn loyal, Frances," he said. "The way you say that makes me think you did know it. Doc Allen told me. He called up a minute ago and he told me to ask you to go out and call on Elise as if nothing happened. See what I mean? She tried to poison herself about two hours ago and her maid found her and called Allen, see? And Allen thinks she ought to have some friend stay out there with her till she gets over this, so I told him you'd be only too glad to go. . . . Well, aren't you going to say anything?"

"I said all right. I'll go," she said, and hung up. She walked across the room and looked at herself in the mirror. She made a face at herself. "Oh. Oh, you lucky girl. You lucky, lucky girl," she said.

By Way of Yonkers

THE MAN lay on the counterpane on the three-quar-
ter-size iron bed. He lay with his hands clasped
behind his head, and his feet were crossed. Every once
in a while he would move, to rub his beard, to draw his
leg up. The room was not cold enough to make it
worth while to put a blanket over his legs, but it was
not warm enough to lie perfectly still and be altogether
comfortable. The man was wearing a pair of gray trousers, brown shoes, and a white shirt with brown stripes.
The shirt was open at the collar. His belt was loosened
but not unbuckled. He lay there with his eyes open,
contemplating the picture of the frightened young
princes in the Tower. "I'll bet they got it," he said
aloud.

Without taking the other hand from behind his head,
without moving his head or anything but his right arm,
the man reached over, groped only a little, and got his
right hand on an alarm clock which was on a small high
table beside the bed. He lifted the clock high, at arm's
length, and held it in a position so that he could tell

what time it was without even moving his eyes. In that way the clock went into the same focus as the two little princes in the Tower. At that moment there were three knocks on the door and the man quickly replaced the clock as a woman's voice said, "Knock, knock, who's there?" It was a voice kidding itself, and not unlike the telephone operator saying, "Grand Hotel, good *mor*ning."

"Come in," said the man.

The door was opened and a girl came in. She had on a black cloth coat, gunmetal stockings, black patent-leather pumps, and a Cossack hat. She had a neat, short nose with jigsaw nostrils and her eyes were bright and black and probably the long eyelashes were basically her own. She was a little taller than short, and in a few years she would be fat.

"Am I very late?" she said, still in the Grand Hotel operator voice.

"You must have come by way of Yonkers," he said.

"I didn't have time to tell you when I called you. I wasn't home then. I was out and I called back to see if there were any messages and of course I recognized your number. I called you from a drugstore."

"How'd you do?" he asked.

"Oh—" she said it very high. Then: "All right. Financially. But do we have to talk about it? You and me?" She began taking off her hat and coat. He did not get up off the bed. She went to a closet and hung her coat on a thin wire hanger and put her hat on the shelf, to reach which she had to stand on tiptoe. She ruffled her hair with fan-spread fingers.

"Do you want a drink?" he said.

"I don't know. I don't guess I do. I'm gettin' tired of liquor. I don't know, lately I sort of lost the taste for it. I go to a bar or some place and I, I don't exactly *want* a drink, but I go there through sheer force of habit or something. And then the bartender says what will I have, and I think and think. I say to myself, 'Will I have a *cock*tail?' No. 'How about a *brandy?*' No. 'A Stinger?' No. 'Gin? Beer? Highball?' No. Then I finally end up with a Scotch-and-soda and it's all I can do to finish it. I don't know what it is with me. I used to love to drink, anything."

"You're almost ready for straight liquor," he said. "You better look out."

"Oh, I'm not afraid of liquor. Gambling, that's the only thing I gotta fear. Especially now. I had a horse come in yesterday. Of course I didn't get track odds because like a goddam fool I just didn't insure the bet and this bookie I deal with, he *knows* I always insure my bets as a rule but this time I had a real hot tip from one of my regulars, a party that gets lots of tips but always tells me to lay off the horses and won't ever tell me a thing. But the night before last, he said to me to play this horse, on the nose, but if I bet more than twenty dollars I was to spread it around and not give it all to the same bookie. Well, I only had twenty bucks to spare, so I went to my regular *bookie* and just gave him the money and said on the nose and I didn't insure it. Bott I guess I can't complain."

"You must be in the chips," the man said.

"I would be, but I have some dental work. Look. See this tooth? Perfectly good. Or you'd think so. Well, don't call me later in the week because I gotta have that out. And up here, you can't even see them, but I have about three or four cavities, and my dentist is terribly dear." She laughed a little.

"What's funny?"

"You'll die. He's a nice Jew, about I'd say around thirty-four-five, and whenever I go to him I know he's dying to make a pass at me. Of course he doesn't know anything about me, and he's *very nice*. I went there through a friend of mine I used to know, a very wealthy party, and you know how when you go to a dentist or a doctor they say who sent you, and I gave the name of this wealthy party because he *told* me to, so this dentist, much as he'd like to move right in, I imagine he's afraid to on account of this other party." She put her hand on his ankle and began rubbing it, slowly. "What's with you?" she said. "I missed you. I was wondering what happened to you, you didn't call."

"I've been broke," he said.

"*That's* all right," she said. "*Don't* ever let that stop you from calling. My God, we're old friends by this time."

"*I* know, but."

"Listen, I'm not worried about you sticking me. And what I just told you, about only having twenty bucks to spare. I said to *spare*. I save a certain amount each week and I stick to it. I make myself do it. If I have a bad week, I still manage to save that certain amount. It's the only way. But for you, well, that's different, honestly it is, Bill. Look. New shoes, new dress, and that coat, I only have it 'bout two months and you know what it cost me? Enough to pay the rent on this dump I'll bet for—four tens are forty—two months at least. I buy good things when I buy them. But I also save my money, a certain amount each week. It's positively the only way." Her words came back to her and she was suddenly embarrassed by the sentimental note. "You said you *been* broke. Does that mean you aren't broke now?"

"That's right."

"Job?"

"Mm-hmm. I guess I won't see you again for quite a while."

"Going out of town?" she said.

"Milwaukee, Wisconsin," he said.

"What doing, or shouldn't I ask?"

"It's all right. Selling beer. During pro'bition I used to have a lot of connections out that way and the other day I ran into an old pal of mine. He was just in town for a couple days and I happened to run *into* him. I did him a couple good turns in the old days and now he's right up there. He took one look at me and said, 'Now listen, level with me. You're strictly from hunger, ain't you?' And I stalled, but he knew. Then he wanted to know if I was in any kind of a jam and I told him no, I just didn't seem to be able to make a connection in this town. So to make a long story short, we went out and got drunk together—"

"Why didn't you call me?"

"I never called you when I was drunk *yet*," the man said, suddenly angry. Then: "Anyway, I'm to meet him at his hotel tomorrow and we'll pro'bly take the train together the next day or the day after. Didn't you notice the new suit and stuff when you hung up your coat?"

"I didn't notice," she said. She crossed her legs.

"He gay me an advance. He said a lot of the same boys are in the business out there and it won't take any time at all before I'm back where I was in '28. Of course maybe not as *much* dough as before, but practically no risks to speak of. I wish it wasn't so late. You and I could go out and celebrate. We can go over to this place over on Fifty-fifth Street."

"I don't want to go anywhere," she said. "Any chance you being back in town soon?"

"Well, not right away, honey. First I have to build up my connections again."

"Well, I don't have to tell you, I'm glad for you. It's about time you got a good break." She resumed rubbing his ankle. He put his hand on the top of her head.

"Yeah? You're as good a break as I ever got."

"Ah, Christ, Bill," she said, and fell face down in tears.

Most Gorgeous Thing

I DON'T think I could ever go back to the stage.
You're constituted different than I am, Lucille. I
have to have more and more time to myself. You
know my new contract? Five pictures a year and permission to do one outside picture for another company.
That way I have more lezzure time to myself to do
what I like. What about you? You used to be a great
reader, but I don't see how you do it any more with
eight performances a week, and I think of the reading
you did in Hollywood. I wouldn't of missed "Good-
bye, Mr. Chips!" for anything, but where would I get
time to read if I had a play on Broadway? Oh, I'm
committed to Hollywood. Definitely. Still, in your
case. I was saying just before I left. When I mentioned
that I was going to New York, I said I was going to
see you and we all said the same thing. I know how
you hated it out there, and naturally, the way they
treated you. But I said, "Now that Lucille is in a hit,
watch them try and get her, but I'll bet they won't
get her for any lousy seven-fifty *this* time." You hold

out for fifteen hundred, darling. You can get it. I
believe Eddie MacIllaney. Oh, you never knew him,
did you? He admired your work from ten years ago.
I didn't know him when you were out there, and now,
poor Eddie! He shot himself just before I left, but
he said you could get fifteen hundred easily, and *ought*
to get *five thousand!* . . .

Do you really want to hear about him? Well, there
isn't so much. He was crazy. Towards the end I was
his only friend left in the world, but even so I have to
admit he was crazy. Nobody knew why he committed
suicide. He had a job. I got him a job at the studio
because I didn't want to see him lose his self-respect.
About a year ago I got him this job. It only paid forty
dollars a week, but it was something. It was a sort of a
writing job. I never even knew if he could write, except poetry a long time ago, but on his say-so I got
him this job. It's a kind of a job that I don't know
how to explain it. You see, when they have a classic,
that there isn't any copyright to it, what they do is to
register with the Academy. The company says we want
to produce, say, *Uncle Tom's Cabin* or, uh, *Macbeth*,
and that means they register it with the Academy, and
then they have to put somebody to work on it, otherwise some other company is liable to go ahead with it

and produce it. So what they do is they get somebody like Eddie and pay him forty dollars a week to write a treatment or something, just to be working on it. Of course they never use anything he writes, but it's some kind of a technicality. You know what a screwy place it is. Anything can happen there, and usually *does!* But that's what Eddie did. I got him the job because I felt sorry for him and I didn't want him to lose his self-respect.

People used to wonder why I was so nice to him, but he was grateful, even if he did have funny ways of showing it sometimes. I guess if he hadn't been around forty-five they would of torn my reputation to pieces, but nobody ever thought of Eddie that way. I used to call him up any time I felt like it, four in the morning, and I'd tell him to whip over and cheer me up when I was blue or depressed. He'd come over, and would we get plastered, but he never took advantage of it except once. One night I came home from a party by myself, I mean I came home without an escort, only a married couple, and I wasn't a bit sleepy, so I called Eddie Mac and he came over and we started drinking out in the kitchen, just the two of us, and the first thing I knew Eddie had his arms around me and kissing my neck and God knows what all he wasn't doing, and saying to me, "You're the most gorgeous thing that ever came to this ill-fated town," meaning Hollywood. Imagine! Of course, naturally, I've had to handle a situation like that before. Well, whenever I've had to deal with a situation like that I've always considered the man, and I knew the best way to deal with Eddie Mac was to talk to him sensibly and reason with him. I said to him, "Don't you think you're making a mistake, Eddie?" I said. "Aren't we being a little foolish? In the first place," I said, "I have no feelings like that for you. Couldn't have." I told him how I felt about him, the difference in our ages and how he was twenty-one, old enough to vote at least, when I was born, or maybe not even that. "Let's forget all about it," I said, and I convinced him that it wouldn't do him any good if I did have an affair with him. He'd lose his job and everything, so even if I felt that way about him it was better for *him* if I didn't give in. He was very depressed and all, but he finally saw it my way, and the only unpleasant thing about it was I caught his cold. We went in my pool without any clothes on later, but I'd done that before without catching cold, so I must of got it from him.

He was laid up for a while with a touch of pneumonia after that and couldn't go to work, but to show him I forgave him I went to bat for him at the studio and made them keep him on salary till he got better. Then, after he was up and around, I called him up one night and he came over and it was just like old times. He was the only man I felt really safe with. I like to get good and plastered every three or four months, and it's nice to know you can get somebody to drink with you that you can forget everything and not have to worry the next day about what did I do and all that. You remember how *you* used to worry, Lucille. I told him that, about how you used to worry. We were talking about you, and he was so impressed because you and I were friends, and he said it was nice of me to show the human side of you, because he'd always thought of you as some kind of a cold idol, like. But anyway—uh—oh, yes, when he was sick. No, I did tell you that. It was when he got better, and this night he came over and we had our first good binge, and that was the last time I saw him alive or at all. I can't bear to look at a dead person, so I never saw him again after that night. He went home, and then a few days later a man came to my house and he said he was Eddie's doctor and I thought he came about the bill, so I said send him in, and he came in and I

said was there any trouble about the bill, because if
there was I'd pay it, and he said well, it wasn't that
exactly. He said he was perfectly willing to let the bill
ride, because he went to college with Eddie, but he
said what he wanted to talk about (and I knew it was
something screwy), he wanted to ask me if I would
help Eddie in a more important way, and I answered
him by saying I'd probably done more for Eddie than
a lot of people he went to college with, and this bird
said yes, but would I do more, and I said that depends. I thought it was going to be some kind of a
shake. Well, what he wanted, he wanted me to make
Eddie go on the wagon. He said if Eddie drank any
more he'd probably keel over and die. Well, what's
that got to do with me, I said. Was I responsible for
a man old enough to be my father? Did I start him
drinking, I said. Didn't Eddie ever hear of liquor before me? I was furious at Eddie and this punk doctor.
I called my butler, and right in front of this person
I gave orders that if Mr. MacIllaney phoned I wasn't
in, no matter what circumstances. "You'll regret this
meddlesome tactics," I said, and then I said if that
concluded his visit, I was busy and he walked out, and
I'll bet he went right back and made up some story
to Eddie, because Eddie phoned that night, but I

wouldn't talk to him. I wanted to prove to this doctor that Eddie drank of his own accord and not because I made him. So of course people came and told me how they saw Eddie plastered all over the place, and then one morning I picked up the papers and big headlines about him committing suicide one afternoon in his office at the studio, otherwise they wouldn't of made such a fuss about it, because Eddie wasn't well known. But people that think I'm cold and aloof, they should of seen me when I read about Eddie doing the Dutch. I couldn't sleep for a week without taking something. He might have bored you, Lucille, but I wish you could of know him slightly. Poor thing, he loved the theatre and New York. He was always going to write a play for me.

Oh, before I forget it. Are you going to Morocco Saturday? I'll get Arthur to get someone for you if you want to.

A Day Like Today

YES, THIS was the right place. It looked more
broken-down in the daylight, but the girl who
was named Sallie remembered the vivid blue shutters
and striping along the corners of the building, and the
steps at the side porch. It looked different in the daylight, but it was the same place, all right. She parked
the car and went inside. A waitress came to her table,
and she ordered a Coca-Cola and some cigarettes. "You
gotta get them out of the machine," the waitress said.
"Over there by the door." The waitress did not leave.
She said, "Will there be somebody with you, because
we don't serve ladies without an escort."

"I'm meeting someone," said Sallie. She *hoped* she
was meeting someone. The waitress went to get the
Coca-Cola.

A man came to the door that opened into the bar
—it was open now. He looked in at her. Another man
did the same thing. Then she knew that a third man
was looking at her, but she kept her eyes on the table.
But this man came in, and it was he. "Hello," he said.

"Hello."

"I'm not late, am I?"

"No. I just got here." She saw that he was wearing his golf clothes. "I see you didn't change," she said.

"No, I came as soon as I finished playing. I was playing in a tournament." He ordered a drink.

"I saw you," she said.

"Oh, were you at the club?"

"Till just a few minutes ago," she said. "I saw you at the seventeenth green and then I left and came here."

"I wondered how you knew I hadn't changed."

"That's how," she said. "I have something of yours." She handed him a gold cigarette case. "This."

"Oh, thanks," he said. "Did I leave it in your car?"

"You left it here, or you would have left it here. On that table over there."

"Is that where we sat?" he asked. "Yes, that's right, we did sit there."

"It's a beautiful case."

"I'm going to give you one like it," he said. "You deserve it."

"Perhaps I do, but don't give me one like it. I wouldn't be able to explain how I got it."

"I don't see why not. Couldn't one of your friends give you one?"

"Not one like that. Practically all my friends are in college, getting small allowances. How could they afford a cigarette case like that on ten or fifteen dollars a week?"

"You're pretty smart," he said. "Well, I'll figure out some way."

"If you do, what will you have engraved in it? Not what you have in that one."

"Of course not. This was given to me."

"I know. By your wife. You didn't tell me you were married. I didn't know it till after I got home and looked inside the case."

He frowned. "Why didn't you give it to me last night?"

"Huh. You wanted to give it to the waiter. And he would have taken it, too." She became angry. "Why? Do you think I kept it so I'd have an excuse to see you? The nerve."

He laughed. "No, Sallie, I didn't think that."

"At least you remember my name. That's something." She refused to let him light a cigarette for her. "Be grateful for small favors," she said.

"Do you remember *my* name?"

"Certainly. Didn't I just see it in the case? Your signature, and June something, 1932. Is that when you were married?"

"Right."

"And your wife's name is Josephine."

"Yes, but how did you know my wife gave it to me?"

"I just guessed. I don't want another Coca-Cola. I'd rather have a Tom Collins or a beer. A beer."

"Two Tom Collins," he said. "You think I'm pretty much of a heel, don't you?"

"What difference does it make what I think? I'm leaving here Tuesday and I'll never see you again."

"What makes you think you'll never see me again? It's a small world. Where do you live?"

"Springfield, Mass."

"Well, don't tell me you never come to New York."

"I'll never tell you if I *do* come to New York. Do you always drink so much? I mean, is last night typical?"

"I don't know," he said. "It's typical of when I'm that tight."

"Do you always cut in on young girls, and—so on?"

"No. Not always. I used to do it a lot about ten

years ago, but they didn't seem so young then. Or so
nice."

"Oh, thank you so much, Mr. Ewing."

"Listen, will you relax and take that chip off your
shoulder? I came here for two reasons. I wanted to
see you again, and I wanted to tell you how sorry I
am about last night."

"What do you remember about last night?"

"What do you think I remember about last night?
I'm sorry about the way it happened. I mean, I'm
sorry about the *way* it happened. I'm not sorry it happened."

She chewed her lower lip. "I'd just as soon you
forgot about last night."

"Oh, don't worry."

"Don't worry! What do you think I am, you . . ."
The waitress slapped the drinks down. "Did you have
a good game?"

"Not bad. I won, one up," he said. The waitress
waddled away.

"One up is good. You must have had harder com-
petition today than last night. I think I'll go now,"
she said. She stood up. He took her hand.

"No, please don't go. Not unless you promise you'll
see me tonight. Are you going to the Chases' party?"

"Yes, but I won't know you. My aunt asked me how I got home last night and I got away with it, but I wouldn't be able to again, and anyway she doesn't like you."

"I hardly know her."

"At lunch she said to my uncle, 'Well, that Jim Ewing made an exhibition of himself again last night. If I were Josephine I'd divorce him.' So I guess last night *was* typical. *Please* let go of my hand."

"I'll see you tonight. It's going to be a huge party. It'll be easy, and I'll stay sober."

"No. Oh, all right, all right. But let me go now."

"I will if you kiss me."

She kissed him, and for one who was really pleading her eyes were curiously angry. "We've got to be careful, Jim. *You* be careful. I don't know how. Good-by."

She went out and he heard the car. He sat there a long time, drinking all of two and part of a third Tom Collins, and then he went to the phone booth. "Speak to Mrs. Ewing. This is Mr. Ewing, Ellen. Tell Mrs. Ewing I'd like to speak to her. . . . Listen, what about not going to this thing at the Chases' tonight? I can't face another day like today."

The Ideal Man

BREAKFAST in the Jenssen home was not much different from breakfast in a couple of hundred thousand homes in the Greater City. Walter Jenssen had his paper propped up against the vinegar cruet and the sugar bowl. He read expertly, not even taking his eyes off the printed page when he raised his coffee cup to his mouth. Paul Jenssen, seven going on eight, was eating his hot cereal, which had to be sweetened heavily to get him to touch it. Myrna L. Jenssen, Walter's five-year-old daughter, was scratching her towhead with her left hand while she fed herself with her right. Myrna, too, was expert in her fashion: she would put the spoon in her mouth, slide the cereal off, and bring out the spoon upside down. Elsie Jenssen (Mrs. Walter) had stopped eating momentarily the better to explore with her tongue a bicuspid that seriously needed attention. That was the only thing she held against the kids—what having them had done to her teeth. Everybody'd warned her, but she wanted—

"Holy hell!" exclaimed Walter Jenssen. He

slammed down his coffee cup, splashing the contents on the tablecloth.

"What kind of talk is that in front of the children?" said Elsie.

"In front of the children! A hell of a fine one you are to be worrying about the children," said Walter. "Just take a look at this. Take a *look* at it!" He handed her the paper as though he were stabbing her with it.

She took the paper. Her eyes roved about the page and stopped. "Oh, *that?* Well, I'd like to know what's wrong with that. Hereafter I'll thank you to keep your cursing and swearing—"

"You! You!" said Walter.

"Myrna, Paul, off to school. Get your coats and hats and bring them in here. Hurry now," said Elsie. The children got up and went to the hall. "Just hold your temper till the children are where they won't hear you, with your raving like somebody *in*sane." She buttoned Myrna's coat and made Paul button his and warned him to keep it buttoned and warned Myrna not to let go of Paul's hand; then she shooed them off with a smile that would have been approved by the Good Housekeeping Institute. But as soon as they were out of the apartment, the smile was gone. "All right, you big baboon, go ahead and curse your head off. I'm used to it."

Walter said, "Gimme back that paper."

"You can have it," said Elsie. She handed him the paper. "Go ahead, read it till you get a stroke. You oughta see yourself."

Walter began to read aloud. " 'Is your husband as attentive to you now that you are married as when he was courting you? Answer: Mrs. Elsie Jenssen, West 174th Street, housewife: Yes, in fact more so. Before we were married my husband was not exactly what would be called the romantic type. He was definitely shy. However, since our marriage he has become the ideal man from the romantic point of view. None of your Tyrone Powers or Clark Gables for me.' For God's sake!"

"Well, so what?" said Elsie.

"So *what?* Do you think that's funny or something? What the hell kind of a thing is that you're putting in the paper? Go around blabbing private matters. I guess all the neighbors know how much we owe on the car. I suppose you tell everybody how much I get. How do you think a person's going to have any self-respect if you go running around and shooting off your face to newspaper reporters?"

"I didn't go around anywhere. He stopped me."

"Who stopped you?"

"The reporter. On Columbus Circle. I was just coming around the corner and he came up and tipped his hat like a gentleman and asked me. It says so there."

Walter wasn't listening. "The office," he said. "Oh, God. What they're going to do to me at that office. McGonigle. Jeffries. Hall. Wait'll they see it. They prob'ly read it already. I can just see them waiting till I get in. I go to my desk and then they all start calling me Tyrone Power and Clark Gable." He stared at her. "You know what's gonna happen, don't you? They'll start kidding till they get too loud, and the boss'll want to know what it's all about, and he'll find out. Maybe they won't come right out and snitch, but he'll find out. And he'll call me in his office and say I'm fired, and he'll be right. I oughta be fired. Listen, when you work for a finance corporation you don't want your employees going around getting a lot of silly publicity. What happens to the public confidence if—"

"It doesn't say a word about you. It says Elsie Jenssen. It doesn't say where you work or anything else. You look in the phone book and there's any number of Walter Jenssens."

"Three, including Queens, too."

"Well, it could be another one."

"Not living on 174th Street. Even if the public doesn't know, they'll know at the office. What if they don't care about the publicity part? All the boss'll want to know is I have a wife that—that goes blabbing around, and believe you me, they don't want employees with wives that go blabbing around. The public—"

"Oh, you and the public."

"Yes, me and the public. This paper has a circulation of two million."

"Oh, hooey," said Elsie, and began to stack the breakfast dishes.

"Hooey. All right, hooey, but I'm not going to that office today. You call up and tell them I have a cold."

"You big baby. If you want to stay home, call them up yourself," said Elsie.

"I said you call them up. I'm not going to that office."

"You go to the office or I'll—who do you think you are, anyway? The time you had off this year. Your uncle's funeral and your brother's wedding. Go ahead, take the day off, take the week off. Let's take a trip around the world. Just quit your job and I'll go back and ask Mr. Fenton to give me back my old job. I'll support you. I'll support you while you sit here, you big baboon." She put down the dishes and put her apron to her eyes and ran out of the room.

Walter took out a cigarette and put it in his mouth but did not light it. He took it out of his mouth and tapped it on the table and lit it. He got up and looked out the window. He stood there a rather long time, with one foot on the radiator and his chin in his hand, looking at the wall across the court. Then he went back to his chair and picked the paper off the floor and began to read.

First he reread his wife's interview, and then for the first time he read the other interviews. There were five others. The first, a laughing Mrs. Bloomberg, Columbus Avenue, housewife, said her husband was so tired when he came home nights that as far as she was concerned romance was only a word in the dictionary.

A Mrs. Petrucelli, East 123rd Street, housewife, said she hadn't noticed any difference between her husband's premarital and present attentiveness. But she had only been married five weeks.

There were three more. The husband of one woman was more attentive, but she did not compare him with Tyrone Power and Clark Gable. The husband of another woman was less attentive, but she did not get sarcastic like Mrs. Bloomberg. The last woman said her husband was radio operator on a ship and she didn't really have much way of telling because she only saw him about every five weeks.

Jenssen studied their photographs, and one thing you had to say for Elsie: she was the prettiest. He read the interviews once more, and he reluctantly admitted that—well, if you had to give an interview, Elsie's was the best. Mrs. Bloomberg's was the worst. He certainly would hate to be Bloomberg when his friends saw that one.

He put down the paper and lit another cigarette and stared at his shoes. He began by feeling sorry for Mr. Bloomberg, who was probably a hard-working guy who really did come home tired. He ended—he ended by beginning to plan what retorts he would have when the gang at the office began to kid him. He began to feel pretty good about it.

He put on his coat and hat and overcoat and then he went to the bedroom. Elsie was lying there, her face deep in the pillow, sobbing.

"Well, I guess I'll go to the office now," he said. She stopped sobbing.

"What?" she said, but did not let him see her face.

"Going downtown now," he said.

"What if they start kidding you?"

"Well, what if they do?" he said.

She sat up. "Are you cross at me any more?" she said.

"Nah, what the hell?" he said.

She smiled and got up and put her arm around his waist and walked down the hall with him to the door. It wasn't a very wide hall, but she kept her arm around him. He opened the door and set his hat on his head. She kissed his cheek and his mouth. He rearranged his hat again. "Well," he said. "See you tonight." It was the first thing that came into his head. He hadn't said *that* in years.

Do You Like It Here?

THE DOOR was open. The door had to be kept open during study period, so there was no knock, and Roberts was startled when a voice he knew and hated said, "Hey, Roberts. Wanted in Van Ness's office." The voice was Hughes'.

"What for?" said Roberts.

"Why don't you go and find out what for, Dopey?" said Hughes.

"Phooey on you," said Roberts.

"Phooey on *you*," said Hughes, and left.

Roberts got up from the desk. He took off his eyeshade and put on a tie and coat. He left the light burning.

Van Ness's office, which was *en suite* with his bedroom, was on the ground floor of the dormitory, and on the way down Roberts wondered what he had done. It got so after a while, after going to so many schools, that you recognized the difference between being "wanted in Somebody's office" and "Somebody wants to see you." If a master wanted to see you on some

minor matter, it didn't always mean that you had to
go to his office; but if it was serious, they always said,
"You're wanted in Somebody's office." That meant
Somebody would be in his office, waiting for you, waiting specially for you. Roberts didn't know why this
difference existed, but it did, all right. Well, all he
could think of was that he had been smoking in the
shower room, but Van Ness never paid much attention
to that. Everybody smoked in the shower room, and
Van Ness never did anything about it unless he just
happened to catch you.

For minor offenses Van Ness would speak to you
when he made his rounds of the rooms during study
period. He would walk slowly down the corridor, looking in at each room to see that the proper occupant,
and no one else, was there; and when he had something to bawl you out about, something unimportant,
he would consult a list he carried, and he would stop
in and bawl you out about it and tell you what punish-
ment went with it. That was another detail that made
the summons to the office a little scary.

Roberts knocked on Van Ness's half-open door and
a voice said, "Come in."

Van Ness was sitting at his typewriter, which was
on a small desk beside the large desk. He was in a

swivel chair and when he saw Roberts he swung around, putting himself behind the large desk, like a damn judge.

He had his pipe in his mouth and he seemed to look over the steel rims of his spectacles. The light caught his Phi Beta Kappa key, which momentarily gleamed as though it had diamonds in it.

"Hughes said you wanted me to report here," said Roberts.

"I did," said Van Ness. He took his pipe out of his mouth and began slowly to knock the bowl empty as he repeated, "I did." He finished emptying his pipe before he again spoke. He took a long time about it, and Roberts, from his years of experience, recognized that as torture tactics. They always made you wait to scare you. It was sort of like the third degree. The horrible damn thing was that it always did scare you a little, even when you were used to it.

Van Ness leaned back in his chair and stared through his glasses at Roberts. He cleared his throat. "You can sit down," he said.

"Yes, sir," said Roberts. He sat down and again Van Ness made him wait.

"Roberts, you've been here now how long—five weeks?"

"A little over. About six."

"About six weeks," said Van Ness. "Since the seventh of January. Six weeks. Strange. Strange. Six weeks, and I really don't know a thing about you. Not much, at any rate. Roberts, tell me a little about yourself."

"How do you mean, Mister?"

"How do I mean? Well—about your life, before you decided to honor us with your presence. Where you came from, what you did, why you went to so many schools, so on."

"Well, I don't know."

"Oh, now. Now, Roberts. Don't let your natural modesty overcome the autobiographical urge. Shut the door."

Roberts got up and closed the door.

"Good," said Van Ness. "Now, proceed with this— uh—dossier. Give me the—huh—huh—*lowdown* on Roberts, Humphrey, Second Form, McAllister Memorial Hall, et cetera."

Roberts, Humphrey, sat down and felt the knot of his tie. "Well, I don't know. I was born at West Point, New York. My father was a first lieutenant then and he's a major now. My father and mother and I lived in a lot of places because he was in the Army and they transferred him. Is that the kind of stuff you want, Mister?"

"Proceed, proceed. I'll tell you when I want you to —uh—halt." Van Ness seemed to think that was funny, that "halt."

"Well, I didn't go to a regular school till I was ten. My mother got a divorce from my father and I went to school in San Francisco. I only stayed there a year because my mother got married again and we moved to Chicago, Illinois."

"Chicago, Illinois! Well, a little geography thrown in, eh, Roberts? Gratuitously. Thank you. Proceed."

"Well, so then we stayed there about two years and then we moved back East, and my stepfather is a certified public accountant and we moved around a lot."

"Peripatetic, eh, Roberts?"

"I guess so. I don't exactly know what that means." Roberts paused.

"Go on, go on."

"Well, so I just went to a lot of schools, some day and some boarding. All that's written down on my application blank here. I had to put it all down on account of my credits."

"Correct. A very imposing list it is, too, Roberts, a very imposing list. Ah, to travel as you have. Switzerland. How I've regretted not having gone to school in Switzerland. Did you like it there?"

"I was only there about three months. I liked it all right, I guess."

"And do you like it here, Roberts?"

"Sure."

"You do? You're sure of that? You wouldn't want to change anything?"

"Oh, I wouldn't say that, not about any school."

"Indeed," said Van Ness. "With your vast experience, naturally you would be quite an authority on matters educational. I suppose you have many theories as to the strength and weaknesses inherent in the modern educational systems."

"I don't know. I just—I don't know. Some schools are better than others. At least I like some better than others."

"Of course. Of course." Van Ness seemed to be thinking about something. He leaned back in his swivel chair and gazed at the ceiling. He put his hands in his pants pockets and then suddenly he leaned forward. The chair came down and Van Ness's belly was hard against the desk and his arm was stretched out on the desk, full length, fist closed.

"Roberts! Did you ever see this before? Answer

me!" Van Ness's voice was hard. He opened his fist, and in it was a wristwatch.

Roberts looked down at the watch. "No, I don't think so," he said. He was glad to be able to say it truthfully.

Van Ness continued to hold out his hand, with the wristwatch lying in the palm. He held out his hand a long time, fifteen seconds at least, without saying anything. Then he turned his hand over and allowed the watch to slip onto the desk. He resumed his normal position in the chair. He picked up his pipe, slowly filled it, and lit it. He shook the match back and forth long after the flame had gone. He swung around a little in his chair and looked at the wall, away from Roberts. "As a boy I spent six years at this school. My brothers, my two brothers, went to this school. My *father* went to this school. I have a deep and abiding and lasting affection for this school. I have been a member of the faculty of this school for more than a decade. I like to think that I am part of this school, that in some small measure I have assisted in its progress. I like to think of it as more than a mere stepping-stone to higher education. At this very moment there are in this school the sons of men who were my classmates. I have not been without my opportunities to take a post at this and that college or university, but I choose to remain here. Why? Why? Because I love this place. I love this place, Roberts. I cherish its traditions. I cherish its good name." He paused, and turned to Roberts. "Roberts, there is no room here for a thief!"

Roberts did not speak.

"There is no room here for a thief, I said!"

"Yes, sir."

Van Ness picked up the watch without looking at it. He held it a few inches above the desk. "This miserable watch was stolen last Friday afternoon, more than likely during the basketball game. As soon as the theft was reported to me I immediately instituted a search for it. My search was unsuccessful. Sometime Monday afternoon the watch was put here, here in my rooms. When I returned here after classes Monday afternoon, this watch was lying on my desk. Why? Because the contemptible rat who stole it knew that I had instituted the search, and like the rat he is, he turned yellow and returned the watch to me. Whoever it is, he kept an entire dormitory under a loathsome suspicion. I say to you, I do not know who stole this watch or who returned it to my rooms. But by God, Roberts, I'm going to find out, if it's the last thing I do. If it's the last thing I do. That's all, Roberts. You may go." Van Ness sat back, almost breathless.

Roberts stood up. "I give you my word of honor, I—"

"I said you may go!" said Van Ness.

Roberts was not sure whether to leave the door open or to close it, but he did not ask. He left it open.

He went up the stairs to his room. He went in and took off his coat and tie, and sat on the bed. Over and over again, first violently, then weakly, he said it, "The bastard, the dirty bastard."